ALICIA CROFTON

Coffee, My Love

A Novel

3DIMPLES
PUBLISHING

First published by Three Dimples Publishing 2019

This novel is entirely a work of fiction. The names, characters and incidents portrayed in it are the work of the author's imagination. Any resemblance to actual persons, living or dead, events or localities is entirely coincidental.

Alicia Crofton asserts the moral right to be identified as the author of this work.

First edition

ISBN: 978-1-7333994-4-9

Cover art by Erik Ebeling
Editing by Alexandra Ott
Proofreading by Beth Attwood

This book was professionally typeset on Reedsy.
Find out more at reedsy.com

To my muse, with love.

Chapter 1

Luca stepped onto the front porch overlooking the coffee fields hidden underneath a thick, rolling fog. The sun glowed behind the distant mountains. Soft rain echoed through the valley, startling the birds as they flew to escape their early morning bath.

The smell of freshly brewed coffee invited him to press his lips against his mug. Luca soaked in the steam, warming his nose before taking his first sip. Rich hints of dark chocolate and mandarin orange danced along his mouth. A lingering bitterness on his tongue left him wondering if the beans had been roasted a touch too long.

Like a king overseeing his kingdom, he leaned on the porch, resting his boot on the lower beam. The fog slowly dissipated into the air, and the sun began to shine over the luscious coffee trees, illuminating the bright red cherries ready to be picked.

Footsteps sounded on the gravel path that connected his brother's house to the plantation. Juan and Mateo were wiping the sleep out of their eyes, their hair unkempt. The twins put on their baskets, loosely attached around their slim teenage waists, and waved to Luca before walking down the hill and settling in front of a tree bursting with red cherries. Luca's other nephew, Fernando, jogged down the gravel road.

At seventeen years old, Fernando had acquired the Mendoza frame—tall and lean, with large squared shoulders. Fernando looked up to meet Luca's glare and ran his fingers through his hair before placing a baseball cap on his head.

"You're late," Luca said.

"Lo siento, Tio. These two knuckleheads wouldn't get out of bed."

Luca and Fernando looked toward the fields, where Juan and Mateo were fighting over the same tree. Elbows were flying. The leaves of the tree were rustling.

"Move it!" Juan cried.

"You move it!" Mateo snapped back.

"Break it up, you two!" Luca called. He shook his head at the fifteen-year-olds, wondering when they were going to act their age.

"Did you happen to get the mail yesterday?" Fernando asked as he scratched the back of his head.

"Sí. Why do you ask?"

"Anything for me?"

"Are you expecting something?"

"No, not really." Fernando looked away. He'd started toward the field when Luca called his name, stopping him in his tracks.

"What are you expecting?"

"A letter!" Juan interrupted.

"From his *girlfriend*!"Mateo added.

Juan and Mateo made kissing sounds and pretended to fondle the coffee trees in front of them, followed by snickering laughter.

"Shut up!" Fernando barked.

Luca tried not to smile.

"All right, all right. Get back to work!" Luca crossed his

arms. "That means you too, *Romeo.*"

"I hate you guys," Fernando said sarcastically as he jogged to the opposite end of the field.

Luca set his coffee mug on the table beside him and pursed his lips. His two youngest nephews were joking around too much. Not enough cherries had made it to their baskets. Luca let out a sharp whistle through his teeth. The twins perked their heads up and stood at full attention. Luca beckoned them to come to the porch, and they both unhooked their baskets. Juan and Mateo stampeded toward Luca like a pair of wild boars, tripping and pulling each other in every direction as they raced up the hill.

"All right," Luca whispered as he motioned with both of his hands to calm them down. "Since you two little devils aren't getting any work done, why don't you tell me what's going on?" Luca brushed his nose with his index finger, trying to hide his mischievous grin. "Who is the girlfriend?"

***

Luca turned the faucet and waited for the rusty brown water to turn clear. Cupping his hands together, he splashed the cool water on his face.

Grabbing his white long-sleeved shirt, he threw it over his head. The thin fabric clung to the post-shower moisture on his back. He stood in front of the mirror for a moment, thinking of how he was going to tell his brother the news. The lines around his mouth deepened at the thought of upsetting Raphael.

Luca walked into the small kitchen. Dishes had piled up in the sink from the past couple of nights eating alone. Empty beer bottles had collected on the counter. The place was a mess.

He poured himself another cup of coffee. As he raised the mug to his lips, he looked up to a pair of dark, angry eyes staring back at him.

"Jesus!" Luca started, spilling hot coffee on his clean white shirt. "Raphael. You scared the crap out of me." Luca looked down at the stain. "Dammit."

Raphael stumbled from the shadows of the living room into the ray of light that poured in from the small window above the sink. As the sunbeam touched Raphael's face, Luca recognized the familiar agitated frown. His tightly wound curls were in complete disarray, the stubble on his face was overgrown, and his shirt was only partially tucked behind the belt that held up his jeans. Alcohol wafted from Luca's brother's pores. It had become an unfortunate and predictable scent. This morning, the smell seemed to be stronger than usual.

"What's going on? Why are you lurking in the shadows of my house?" Luca asked as he nervously brushed by him.

"Do you know why my boys didn't look me in the eye this morning? They are up to something," Raphael sneered. He impatiently tapped the ring on his finger against his brass belt buckle.

"Raphael," Luca said. "Take it easy." Luca knew that he needed to ease his brother into the news. Raphael's temper was wild and unpredictable when he was sober, and far worse when he was drunk. "Do you remember when we were teenagers? And we used to ride our bikes to the market across town?"

Raphael nodded, furrowing his brow.

"We convinced that cute store clerk to sell us beer."

"I remember. You could have charmed her right out of her uniform." Raphael smiled as he looked into the distance, probably searching through the memories still lingering somewhere in his drunken state of mind.

Luca relaxed.

"What was her name again?" Raphael asked.

"Lucita, I think it was." Luca smiled back, remembering the skinny young girl who could tear through a metal can with her two front teeth.

"Ah, yes." Raphael sighed. "Lu-ci-ta." He grinned.

Luca chuckled.

"What does this have to do with my boys?" Raphael asked abruptly.

"Well, one of your boys must have acquired some of my charm," Luca said with a proud smile.

"Qué?" Raphael asked, clearly growing impatient.

"I believe Fernando has a girlfriend," Luca said, raising an eyebrow. "You can't blame him. He's got my chiseled jaw and my godlike physique." Luca chuckled.

"Girlfriend?" Raphael asked, blowing his hair out of his eyes. "Is that why Juan and Mateo have been avoiding me?"

Luca frowned. "It's a little more complicated than that, actually."

"How do you mean?"

"Fernando's girlfriend," Luca said cautiously, putting his hands on his brother's shoulders. "His girlfriend's name is Luisa. Luisa *Santiago*."

"What?!" Raphael barked, shoving Luca's hands away. "He's dating a Santiago?"

"Raphael," Luca pleaded with his brother. "She had nothing to do with the—"

"No!" Raphael shouted. "That traitorous piece of shit!"

Raphael grabbed the coffee mug on the counter and slammed

it to the floor, splattering more coffee on Luca's white shirt. Ceramic pieces scattered across the room.

"Tranquila. Tranquila!" Luca wrapped his arms around his brother while he thrashed about, struggling in vain to escape Luca's grasp. Luca gripped him tighter, moving him toward the living room floor.

"Calma," Luca whispered. "Calma, Raphael."

Raphael eventually became limp in Luca's arms. Luca slowly loosened his grip as he felt his brother's muscles relax.

"Carina," Raphael stuttered with a quivering lip. "My poor Carina." He shook as he sobbed into Luca's shoulder. "She wasn't supposed to—"

"I know," Luca whispered back as he guided his brother to the worn, plaid sofa in the dusty living room. "I know, mi hermano ..."

He helped his brother lie down, then grabbed a cream-colored knit blanket nearby and gently laid it over him.

"Mi amor," Raphael wailed as he turned his head into the back of the couch, still shaking with silent sobs.

Luca lost track of time as he sat on the edge of the couch, trying to lull Raphael to sleep by rubbing his back like their mother used to. When Raphael's breathing slowed to a steady rhythm, Luca tiptoed out the front door.

A pack of Marlboro Lights and a green pocket lighter beckoned for him on the side table resting against the porch railing. Luca grabbed the pack and popped a single cigarette with a flick of his wrist. He lit it and took a long, slow draw. *Raphael. What am I going to do with you?*

Before the accident, Raphael had already been unraveling. His mood swings were increasingly violent. His drinking was out of hand. Carina's death only made matters worse for Raphael's mental state. It wasn't until the day Raphael nearly strangled an executive during a negotiation meeting that Raphael was deemed unfit to run the plantation anymore. Somehow Luca talked Raphael into being the office manager, letting him work behind the scenes, but even that amount of responsibility seemed too much for Raphael to handle.

Luca took another long drag of his cigarette. He knew there was a ton of paperwork to be done in the office, but Raphael was in no condition to organize his own thoughts. Luca kicked the railing of his deck, and the shooting pain from the ends of his toes radiated up to his shin.

"Dammit." He put his cigarette out in the ashtray and shook out his throbbing foot. "Guess I'll be working in the office today," he said to himself. He hobbled down the gravel pathway and immersed himself in paperwork while Raphael slept off his hangover.

Chapter 2

The alarm clock blasted through the still morning, startling Emery from her deep slumber. It was four a.m. She was sure she hadn't slept more than a couple of hours after tossing and turning all night. She pulled the white comforter from her legs and placed her feet on the cold wood floor.

Emery tied her running shoes on and pulled her long auburn hair into a high ponytail. She stepped on the treadmill by the large bedroom window that overlooked the sparkling city lights below and began her morning jog.

Today was her first day as the vice president of operations at Coffee Benz Company, her dream job ever since she had written her thesis on fair-trade practices in the coffee industry. After graduating from Kellogg Business School, Emery had sought a position with Coffee Benz because they were the leaders of the fair-trade movement. They had direct relationships with their plantations by cutting out the middlemen and providing fair prices to the coffee farmers.

If she was going to work hard, she wanted to work for a company that was committed to making the world a better place. And so she did. After seven years and five promotions, she'd made it to vice president at only thirty years old. She knew she would have to work extra hard to impress Don Campbell, the CEO, and the male-dominated board of directors, but she was up to the task.

Stepping into the white-tiled shower stall, Emery soaked in the steam, letting the cloak of hot water cascade down her body. She practiced her opening speech for her staff meeting and made a mental checklist of all her big presentations for the day.

Emery chose a cream-colored blouse that buttoned all the way up to the base of her neck, the better to hide the blotchy red spots that appeared when she was nervous. She carefully traced the hemline of her pencil skirt down her hips to ensure everything was in place.

As she gazed into her almond-shaped eyes, she forced a smile and added a touch of blush to her freckled cheekbones. Her hair was pulled back into a tight low bun, not a strand out of place.

Emery straightened her posture in her reflection one last time, doing her best to dismiss any glimmer of self-doubt resting in the back of her mind.

Would the team take her seriously as a leader? She was younger than most of them by at least five years.

"Just be yourself," she whispered under her breath, thinking of the words her father had told her the last time they spoke.

"You're going to be great," Emery's dad had said.

"It's just weird that these people have been my peers for the past year, and now I'm their boss."

"You've always been the boss." Her dad chuckled over the phone. "Now you just have the title to go with it."

"I learned from the best."

"You've built an incredible career for yourself at such a young age. I am so proud of you, Emy."

"Thanks, Dad."

"Oh, hey, Emy," Emery heard muffled voices in the background.

"Do you have to go?"

"Yeah, honey. Mom and I are supposed to meet up with friends."

"Okay, Dad."

"One more thing. Don't forget to be yourself, and I love ya."

"I love you too."

Click.

"Just be yourself," she repeated as she took one last look in the mirror and walked out the door, leaving all her insecurities behind.

***

"Good morning, boss," Jake Whitmore said with a wide smile. His tousled blond hair fell just above his sparkling gray eyes. He perched himself on Emery's desk, holding out a steaming-hot mug. "We just got this batch from one of our new plantations in the north region. It's pretty good."

Emery carefully took the coffee mug and held it to her nose. She examined the color and took a sip. The rich caramel flavor coated her tongue.

"Thank you," Emery said.

"VP looks good on you."

"Well, it feels good. And congratulations to you as well, *Senior* Director of Supply. I hope it won't be too awkward that I'm your boss now."

"Of course it won't be awkward. We'll make a good team.

We always have. See you in a few minutes."

Jake gave Emery a wink and strolled across the hall into his new office. He left a trail of confidence that Emery envied. Jake had been her first manager at Coffee Benz, and he continued to mentor her over the years. At first their relationship was strictly professional, but eventually, they became friends.

Sometimes she wished she was more like him. He was charismatic and fun. He was friends with everybody at the company, including the CEO and half of the senior leadership team. They played golf on weekends, and got together for whiskey and cigars after work. Jake was in with the good ol' boys, and Emery was on the outside looking in.

Through the windowpane of Emery's office, she could see her assistant, Jeanine, casually walk to her desk. Jeanine's high heels clicked against the tile floor, sending echoes from all the way down the hall.

9:05 a.m. *Late.*

Jeanine's red hair was teased into wild curls. Her face was pale, with high cheekbones and long, pointy features. A pair of thin red-rimmed glasses sat at the edge of her nose as she turned on her computer.

"Good morning, Jeanine," Emery called from her office.

"Good morning, Ms. Smith."

Jeanine held her gaze on her computer screen, clicking the keyboard with her fingernails. Not once did she look up to acknowledge her new boss.

Emery had never had an assistant before, but she had envisioned their interaction going a little differently—being on time, for one. Perhaps Jeanine was not a morning person. Emery could try to work around that, even though she personally hated to be late to anything.

"Ms. Smith?" Jeanine's nasal tone interrupted Emery's thoughts. She stood in the doorway with her arms crossed. "Are you planning on attending your staff meeting that started six minutes ago?"

"The meeting started at nine? I thought it was at nine thirty." Flustered, Emery collected the documents she had prepared the night before.

"The meeting got moved to accommodate some of the team's schedules today. Apparently, nine thirty was terribly inconvenient."

Jeanine peered through her glasses, watching Emery attempt to balance her stack of papers in one hand and her coffee mug in the other.

"That would have been nice to know. Do you mind scheduling our next staff meeting so that it is more convenient for everyone, please?"

Jeanine sat back down at her desk, letting Emery's request go unanswered.

Emery huffed down the hall, spilling coffee on her papers and arriving at her first staff meeting eight minutes late.

"Sorry," Emery said as she entered the room. She forced a smile while concealing the building anxiety that pooled in her stomach. "Thank you so much for joining me this morning. I wanted to start by saying that I am so lucky to have such a strong team."

Emery received polite smiles, but the room was silent except for a single cough in the back. The air felt suffocating while Emery tried organizing her coffee-stained papers.

"We are pumped to have you as our fearless leader!" shouted Jake, cutting through the tension of the boardroom. The team sitting around the table chuckled at Jake's outburst.

Emery gave Jake an appreciative grin. Feeling more comfortable, she continued with her first meeting as vice president.

"All right," she called out. "At this time—" Emery was interrupted by two quick knocks at the door before it swung open. Greetings and cheers belted from the room. Emery turned around and, to her astonishment, Jeanine was standing in the doorway. Apparently, Jeanine was well respected among her team. Emery made a mental note to reconsider confronting her about her tardiness earlier.

"Ms. Smith, Jake. I'm sorry to interrupt, but Don Campbell needs a word with the two of you," she reported.

This day was running away from her. Emery took a calming breath and made a stack of her things.

"I guess this means we'll delay our staff meeting until next week. In the meantime, don't hesitate to stop by my desk anytime. My door is always open."

Emery left the room in a haze.

"Don't worry, boss. You've got this," Jake whispered as they both turned the corner toward the elevator.

"I feel frazzled already and it's not even ten a.m."

"You'll get the hang of it."

"I hope so," Emery said as she looked at her reflection in the elevator door and smoothed a loose strand of hair back into place.

"Say now, where's that confidence we've been working so hard to build up?"

"You're right, you're right."

"You're going to need it. Because Don Campbell can smell fear. Don't worry. I've got your back."

✳✳✳

Emery knocked assertively on the door before entering. Don Campbell's office had vaulted ceilings and dark mahogany wood finishes. Tall bronze sculptures stood in every corner, and across the room a series of three large windows overlooked the Chicago skyline.

Don was sifting through a stack of reports cluttered across his desk. His thinning silver-white hair was cut short along the sides of his large, round head. He had gray eyes magnified behind thick reading glasses that he peered through as Emery and Jake walked in.

"I trust you two are getting settled into your new offices?" Don asked.

"Settling in fine, thank you," Emery replied.

"Good. I'm going to get down to business." Don cleared his throat before he continued. "The quarterly financials are coming in below targets. We need to cut supply costs by ten percent to make up lost revenue in the first half of the year."

Don cleared his throat again.

"Excuse me, but did you just say *ten percent*?" Emery asked. "Wouldn't this mean our coffee farmers would be getting paid less than the market average?"

"Sadly, you are correct, my dear," Don reported. "You two are to prepare for a little tour de Colombia to iron out the details."

Emery's face grew warm. Her mouth went dry. A ten percent supply cost reduction would surely put some of the coffee farmers out of business. She wasn't prepared for this kind of task. The whole reason she wanted to work for Coffee Benz in the first place was that they paid their farmers a fair wage, *above* the market average.

"Sir," Emery started.

"I know this is not a simple request," Don mumbled as he picked up a few graphs and held them into the air. "But I know that the two of you can do it. Please make the necessary arrangements, and report back to me once you have made some movement."

Don smiled at the two of them one last time before returning his focus to the papers scattered on his desk. Emery and Jake stood in stunned silence until it was clear their meeting was over. On their way out the door, Don called, "Whitmore, will I see you at the tournament this weekend?"

"Yeah, I'll be there. I'm meeting up with Billy for a drink afterward. Come and join us."

Don nodded gruffly and resumed his desk work.

Emery closed the door behind them and let out the breath she had been holding for what seemed like minutes.

"This isn't right," Emery whispered as she and Jake walked toward the elevator lobby.

"What do you mean? Don and I go way back. He helped me with my golf swing."

"No, I am not talking about men's-only golf club outings. I'm talking about the price cuts."

"Oh right. Yeah, ten percent is a big hit." Jake ran his fingers through his hair.

"There's got to be another way to make back the revenue."

"That's what I like about you, Emery," Jake said as he pressed the bottom button of the elevator pad. "You've got an eye for alternatives."

"Oh, is that what you like about me?"

"That"—Jake grinned—"and you have a great ass—"

"Excuse me?" Emery gasped.

"Astute! An astute eye for business!" Jake cocked his head

back and laughed. "Jeez. You didn't let me finish."

"Shame on you." Emery playfully pushed his shoulder. "This is serious! I don't know what we're going to do."

"Look at the bright side." Jake smiled.

"Oh yeah? And what's that?"

"You just scored a romantic tropical getaway with one of Chicago's most eligible bachelors," Jake said teasingly.

"You are an HR nightmare," Emery scoffed and shooed him back to his office.

Jake was always flirting with everyone, so Emery didn't take it seriously. But now that she was his boss, she would need to tell him to tone down the jokes. She wouldn't want any of the good ol' boys to get the wrong idea about their friendship.

Heat from Jeanine's gaze pricked the back of her neck. When she turned around, she found a very perturbed assistant.

"Is everything okay, Jeanine?"

"You're ten minutes late to your next appointment. Shall I reschedule?"

"Shoot. This day is just getting away from me."

"I can tell," Jeanine sneered.

Emery bit her tongue. She would have to figure out how and why her team gushed over Jeanine earlier. So far, Emery was not impressed.

"Jeanine, please reschedule all my meetings next week and book two round trips to Bogota, Colombia, for Jake and me. We will need to leave first thing on Monday."

"Is this for your romantic tropical getaway with Chicago's most eligible bachelor?"

Emery could feel her skin blush.

"That's not … what you heard … it was just a joke."

"Don't worry, Ms. Smith. Your secret is safe with me."

"But there's no secret."

"Ms. Smith, your meeting?"

"Oh crap. I'm so late."

Emery scurried to her next meeting, spending the rest of her first day as vice president bouncing from one meeting to the next, at least fifteen minutes late and flustered.

Chapter 3

Fernando smiled from ear to ear as he sat on the edge of his bed, rereading the last sentence of his letter from Luisa.

With Love, Always & Forever.

Fernando closed his eyes and lifted the paper to his nose. He smelled traces of the perfume she wore that reminded him of daisies on a summer day. He reveled in the vision of her long, black hair braided over one shoulder, and her perfectly plump lips.

"Fernando!"

Two masculine hands grabbed his shoulders, shaking him out of his daydream. Luca appeared in Fernando's direct line of sight with his arms crossed.

"We need to talk," Uncle Luca said slowly.

"What about?"

"The Santiago girl," his uncle whispered while looking over his shoulder.

Fernando's adrenaline spiked. How did Uncle Luca find out about her? He and Luisa had been so careful not to get caught.

Juan and Mateo. Fernando's hands clenched into fists. His fingernails dug into the skin of his palms.

"Ay," Luca said.

"Please don't tell Dad. You know he won't be able to handle it."

"It's too late. He already knows."

"Shit."

"'Shit' is right. Don't worry about him for now. I've got it under control. Are you serious about this girl? Or is it just a fling?"

Fernando paused for a moment, biting his lip. "I *love* her, Tio."

Luca rested his head in his hands, silently nodding.

"Okay then, maybe it's time I take your father to a therapist. He's going to need to get comfortable with the idea of you and Luisa together."

"My father will never go for that." Fernando shook his head.

"I'll think of something then," Uncle Luca said, taking out a cigarette.

"Gracias, Tio."

Ever since their mother died and their father completely fell to pieces, Luca had filled the void in their lives, acting as the responsible adult in the family. He was practically raising the boys on his own while their father lay passed out on the couch most of the day. If it wasn't for their uncle, the boys wouldn't have groceries in the fridge or a place to stay when their father was on a dangerous tirade.

His uncle squeezed his shoulder before releasing it. "It's going to be fine. One day Luisa will be sitting at the family dinner table with all of us."

Fernando nodded, but he couldn't help his feelings of doubt.

"I'll get back to work," Fernando said, heading toward the doorway.

Uncle Luca nodded and moved out of the way so that

Fernando could walk by.

"Fernando?"

Fernando froze midstep.

"Where's the rest of the mail?"

***

Luca sat down in the wooden chair at his desk. It creaked and growled as Luca settled in and observed the overwhelming mess. Envelopes were strewn across it, but there was one envelope that caught his attention. He stared at the red-and-blue-striped edges. It was a letter from Coffee Benz.

The last time Luca and Raphael had received a letter like this was a couple of years ago, when they were informed there would be meetings to discuss the new terms of agreement.

It felt like only yesterday Luca was peeling Raphael off one of the Coffee Benz executives, prying Raphael's hands loose from the man's neck. He had turned into an animal that day. It was the last time Raphael was allowed to attend a business meeting, and the first time Luca realized Raphael's condition had become serious.

Luca held a brass letter opener in one hand and nervously tapped it on the edge of the desk. With a flick of the wrist, he cut through the envelope to open it and pulled out the corporate memo. His eyes darted from word to word as his heartbeat spiked.

"No," Luca hissed under his breath. They wanted to set up renegotiations, again.

Luca threw the document on the table in disgust. He brought his hands to his temples and rubbed the throbbing pain that had built up since that morning. What was he going to do?

He snatched the letter back from the table and searched the document for a name. At the bottom of the page was an illegible signature sitting above the small print: Emerson Smith, VP of operations, Coffee Benz Company.

Luca traced his lips with his finger. Maybe he could find this *Emerson Smith* and talk some sense into the man before the negotiations started. If the man had a heart at all, he would reconsider.

Laughter in the distance echoed off the windowpanes from outside the office. He stood to look out the window and found his twin nephews tumbling in the yard. Fernando approached them, laughing at his brothers as they smeared mud in each other's faces. Fernando's laugh turned into a cough, but he looked happy. They were all happy.

Luca crumpled the letter in his hand with a tight fist. He would do whatever was necessary to keep the plantation and prevent the family from slipping into poverty. He had to make a plan.

Like a madman, Luca tore through his office to find Mr. Bolton's number. He was the one who helped Luca get out of the mess after "the incident." And he was also the one who convinced his boss not to press charges against Raphael. Maybe he could help. He had to help!

Business cards and files flew in a tornado of paper.

"Found you," Luca said, holding a business card that was stained and frayed around the edges. Luca grabbed the office hands-free phone and carefully dialed the phone number.

While the phone rang, he cracked the office door open and peered into the living room. Raphael was still sleeping on the couch. His arms were extended above his head, and the blanket Luca had placed on him was dangling onto the floor.

"Jake Whitmore speaking."

Luca looked at the phone as if it had played a joke on him.

"I'm sorry, I thought this was Mr. Bolton's number."

"Ah, Mr. Bolton no longer works for the company. I'm the new senior director of supply now."

"Yake, was it?"

"It's Jake, not Yake."

"My name is Luca Mendoza from the Colombian Coffee Plantation. I am hoping to speak with Emerson—"

"I see. You're calling to make arrangements for the negotiations?"

"Yes, well, no. If I could just talk with Emerson—"

"Luke, was it? Let me transfer you over to Jeanine. She will get you squared away."

"It's Luca—"

Click.

The sound of jazz saxophone filled the line while Luca flared his nostrils. When the phone picked up, smacking sounds of chewing gum was followed by a nasal voice. "Good afternoon, Emerson Smith's office. How can I serve you today?"

"My name is Luca Mendoza with the Colombian Coffee Plantation and I—"

"Mr. Mendoza, we have already scheduled the negotiation meetings for next week. If you'd like, I can pencil you in on Friday at eleven a.m. in the Medellín office."

"Yes, about that. I was wondering if I could speak with Emerson first."

"Unfortunately, that will not be possible. I suggest you pick a time slot now. Would you like to take the eleven a.m. or would you rather call back another time?"

"I just really need to talk with—"

"I'm going to put you down for Friday at eleven. And if you need to reschedule, you can call back another time. Have a nice day, Mr. Mendoza."

Clunk.

Luca looked at the phone in a fury of disbelief. *Did she just hang up?* He put the phone back to his ear to check and was surprised when he heard muffled sounds. He pressed his ear harder against the phone, and the nasal voice started again.

"Mmm mmm … Do you want to attend the gala event during the festival or not? You fly in the same day."

There was a pause. Luca held his breath.

"I'll call them right now to let them know you plan to attend."

Was Jeanine talking to Emerson? There was a good chance she was, and if she was, Emerson was going to be at a gala the night of the festival. The Feria de Las Flores was happening that week. That had to be what she was talking about.

Luca plopped back down in his chair, his mind racing. If he could sneak into the gala and find Emerson, he could convince him to come back to the plantation. He would see for himself there was no more room to cut costs.

"What are you doing?" Raphael asked, his voice scratchy and dry from sleeping with his mouth open.

Luca almost fell out of his chair.

"Ay! You really need to stop sneaking up like that!"

Raphael let out a forced laugh.

"Since you're here," Luca began, "there's something we need to talk about." He motioned for his brother to take a seat in the metal chair across from his desk. "I need to go into the city for a couple of days."

"Why?"

Luca adjusted his tone and straightened his position in his

chair. "There's a new VP of operations at Coffee Benz, and I'd like to bring him here to visit our plantation."

"For what? What good will that do?"

Luca locked eyes with his brother.

"It's good for relations," Luca said firmly.

"Whatever you say, *boss*," Raphael said with his hands up. Raphael shifted his weight, pulling a metal flask from his back pocket. He opened the top and took a swig. "You want me to go with you?" Raphael asked.

"No, no. I need you here." Luca motioned with his hands. "I need you to watch over the plantation while I am out. I should be back in a couple of days, hopefully with Mr. Smith, to show him around and give him the friendly Mendoza tour."

"The friendly Mendoza tour." Raphael smiled slyly.

"I need you to be on your best behavior." Luca cocked his eyebrow. "That includes keeping your boys in check without smacking them around."

"Okay, okay. I'll be like the patron Saint Thomas of Aquinas." Raphael crossed his heart and gave Luca a wink.

"Bueno. Gracias." Luca got up and patted Raphael's shoulder. "I leave first thing tomorrow morning."

***

That evening, the air was still. Luca stood on his porch, overlooking the blackened trees in the distance. They did not budge or sway in the breeze. All was quiet except for the pounding of Luca's scheme growing inside his head.

He thought about all the things he would show Emerson if he was willing to take a trip to their humble plantation. He remembered a small batch of coffee that was roasted prior to the last round of cuts. Perhaps he could get Emerson to taste how delicious and rich the coffee used to be, and compare it to the coffee they were making now. Ever since the last round of price cuts, Luca had to find ways to make a profit. He used the cheapest pesticides on the market and had fewer people to help wash and clean the beans. The quality of the beans had deteriorated. He just needed to prove it had to do with the cost reductions.

He took one last drag of his cigarette and slowly exhaled the smoke through his nostrils before going inside. Luca sat in his tattered reclining chair, thinking about how he was going to find which gala Emerson would be at, when a soft knock came from the front door. Although he didn't need to, he found himself peeking through the peephole to confirm who was at the door.

Esmeralda stood on the front porch, softly lit by the glow coming from the living room window. She was fluffing her hair and blotting her red lips. Her three-inch heels concealed the fact that she was less than five feet tall, with long black waves of thick, silky hair. She wore a tight dress cut low at the chest, accentuating the curves of her voluptuous body.

Luca opened the door. "Esmeralda." He sighed as he leaned against the door frame. "What brings you here at this hour?"

Esmeralda looked up to Luca and pouted. "Oh, come on, Luca, don't play dumb with me."

The corner of Luca's mouth curled up as she sauntered through the door.

"This actually isn't a good time."

Esmeralda ignored him and walked toward the kitchen. Ice cubes clinked against glass, and she emerged with two tumblers full of amber-colored liquid.

"Here," she hummed as she raised a glass toward Luca.

"What's this?"

"A little something I picked up from the restaurant. Try it."

Luca pressed the cool glass to his lips and took a sip of the sweet almond flavor.

Esmeralda bit her lower lip in anticipation. "Do you like it?"

"It's not bad."

Luca took a generous gulp, letting the smooth burn warm his belly.

Esmeralda took the glass from his hand and placed it on the island counter behind her. Grabbing his hand, she playfully dipped his index finger into her drink. It was ice cold. She swirled his fingertip around the glass and then slowly brought his finger up to her mouth. She traced the edges of her plump lips with his dripping finger before slowly inserting it into her warm, wet mouth. She closed her lips around his knuckle and let her tongue roll around as she sucked the liquor from his fingertip.

Luca's mouth gaped open as he fell under her spell, mesmerized by the rippling pleasure. Esmeralda looked up through her thick lashes and released his finger.

Triumphantly, she walked toward the bedroom as Luca obediently followed.

Chapter 4

Raphael waved to his brother as he watched Luca drive away in his light blue pickup truck. He rubbed the stubble on his chin as he pondered Luca's sense of urgency to bring the American back to the plantation. The men in suits never came to visit the farm. What made Luca think they would come now?

Back in the office, Raphael looked upon the stacks of paperwork needing to be organized and filed. He instinctively reached toward his back pocket and grabbed his flask. After pouring a healthy amount into a mug of stale coffee, he walked back to the desk, bumping into a small trash can. Crumpled balls of paper fell onto the office floor.

"Dammit," Raphael growled, shoving pieces of paper back into the trash can. One by one, Raphael forced each piece of trash with more and more rage. While reaching for the last of the garbage, his eyes caught the corner of a red-and-blue-striped envelope. Raphael shifted his weight on the floor. He studied the envelope in his hands, trying to think why they would have received a letter from Coffee Benz. He remembered the trouble that had come with a letter like it before.

Raphael pulled himself to his feet and shuffled through

opened letters, searching for anything that looked important.

He found nothing.

He took a step back from the desk and placed his hands on his hips. Underneath the desk was a crinkled letter. Raphael reached toward the floor and pulled it up into the light. It was dated a few days ago from Emerson Smith, VP of operations for Coffee Benz.

Raphael's eyes raced over the letter. His heart stopped over the three words *renegotiating supply costs*, and he found himself ripping it into shreds.

"Those bastards!" he yelled. He slammed his fists onto the desktop. The plantation would not survive another round of budget cuts. They were going to lose their farm.

Raphael dropped into the office chair and put his head in his hands. Luca said that he was going into Medellín to speak with Emerson Smith. He must be trying to handle this on his own. Raphael tightened his fists. A pang of disappointment stung his chest. He had agreed that Luca would be in charge of the business affairs, but that didn't stop Raphael from wanting to contribute to the decisions. He had every right to know what was going on.

If Luca blew it, they would lose everything. Raphael couldn't just sit back and let this happen. He needed to do something. Raphael rushed down the hall into his bedroom and started to gather his things.

"Are you going somewhere?" Fernando interrupted Raphael's flurry. Fernando stood cautiously by the door frame, holding his arms as he watched his father frantically throw a pair of socks into a duffel bag.

"Sí," Raphael said. He turned back to his suitcase and shoved a pair of pants inside. "I'm going to help Luca with some business."

"When will you be back?" Fernando asked, coughing into his elbow.

Raphael turned to pat Fernando on the back, hoping to ease his cough.

"In a couple of days," Raphael said gently. "Will you be able to look after the office while your uncle and I are away?"

Fernando's cough subsided, and he looked directly into his father's eyes and nodded.

Fernando had Carina's eyes. His heart broke for the millionth time. He would never escape the painful memories of his wife, no matter how much he tried.

Raphael's jaw clenched. "Pick up the office while you're at it. File all the paperwork and organize the cabinets."

"But Dad—"

"Just do it!" Raphael snapped. He turned to his luggage and zipped up the contents.

Fernando coughed into his arm. Blotches of red stained his cheeks.

"Are you going to be okay?" Raphael asked.

"It's just a cold. I'm fine," Fernando said between muffled coughs.

"No company while I'm gone, you hear?"

"Of course."

"I know about Luisa."

Fernando froze in terror.

"Dad, I—"

"Save it. We'll handle it when I get back." Raphael stormed out of the house, slamming the door behind him. He kicked a rock before hopping into his rusted orange truck. Peeling out of the driveway, he drove down the long road to the city.

***

Four years ago …

Carina didn't know her husband anymore. There had been a time when Raphael's temper was adorable. His passion was one of the reasons she loved him. However, lately, his moods had become erratic and unpredictable.

Today she had built up the courage to confront him. She wanted everything to go perfectly, so she cleaned the house before he got home from the coffee harvest. The house smelled of seasoned pork while she prepped for Raphael's favorite meal. She even made an extra trip to the store to stock the fridge with his favorite cervezas.

A minute after six o'clock, Raphael lumbered through the kitchen and washed his hands. He grabbed a beer out of the fridge, slamming the door shut. He hunched over the sink with his bottle opener and pried the beer cap until it popped off, clanking on the kitchen counter next to the tray of empanadas.

"What is this? A special occasion or something?" he asked, tilting his head back and guzzling the beer.

"I just wanted to make your favorite," Carina said. "Let's sit and eat. The boys are with Luca tonight. I thought we could talk."

Raphael tilted his eyebrow toward Carina before taking a seat at their kitchen table. He watched her carefully as he finished the last few gulps. A hissing sigh screeched from his mouth as he placed the empty bottle on the table.

Carina took a shaky breath as she served him his plate. Her heart thumped in her ears, and she urged him to eat before she could muster the strength to say what she needed to say.

Raphael's gaze never left Carina as he took a bite of his food.

"It's just that …" Carina started. "You don't seem happy."

"Not this again." Raphael sprang up from his chair, letting it crash behind him. He walked to the refrigerator again and pulled out another beer.

"I think we should see a doctor," Carina said. "I think they might be able to help. Maria told me that—"

"Leave Maria out of this!" Raphael roared, silencing Carina from saying anything more. Raphael lifted the chair from the floor before sitting back down. The air between them was thick.

"Is it me?" Carina asked, a single tear falling down her left cheek. "Are you not happy with me?"

Raphael held his blank stare somewhere between Carina's nose and lips. His jaw clenched before he picked up his plate and smashed it on the ground.

"I'm not going to talk about this anymore!" Raphael yelled.

Carina stormed out, slamming the door shut behind her. The trail of hot tears hit the cool evening air. She stifled the sob in her throat and wiped her face with the back of her hand.

Shouting from inside the house was muted by the screaming of the truck engine struggling to start. The truck jolted forward, and Carina sped down the plantation road, leaving a dust cloud in her wake.

Carina parked her car along the main street and decided to walk. She was convinced she needed to get Raphael some help, but she didn't know how. She longed for the days they used to laugh together. He had been charming and funny when she first met him. He was devilishly handsome too. And when he wanted to be, he was sweet and romantic.

Carina paused to think about the last time he was romantic.

Scouring through her memories, she recalled the time he brought home flowers and whisked her away from the kitchen to slow dance in their living room. They had been so madly in love then. That night must have been over seventeen years ago.

Gravel crunched underneath her feet as she cut through the foggy evening. The road ahead was lit by the silver moonlight above. A sliver of the moon came and went as bustling clouds rolled in from faraway mountains.

Just then, a clearing in the clouds opened the gates of a beautiful starry sky. She stood and looked at the constellations above, twinkling brightly against the deep indigo backdrop. She wished upon the moon and stars for the man she fell in love with to come back to her, to laugh and dance with her again.

Behind her, the rattling sound of a truck came near. Perhaps Raphael had come to take her home. She looked over her shoulder to see two bright headlights, blinding her before the impact.

Raphael had finished his sixth beer by the time the boys got home. They asked for their mother, but Raphael sent them straight to bed, threatening to take out his belt if they didn't listen. He paced the living room floor and paced some more. His patience had run out over an hour ago, and now the electric clock on the wall taunted him with each passing minute. It was eight after ten when the phone rang.

"Hola?"

"Mr. Mendoza?"

"Sí."

"This is Sheriff Sanchez."

Raphael did not respond. The corners of the room grew

dark, closing him into a trap. He couldn't move. He couldn't breathe. He stared down the hallway as each of his sons poked their heads out from their rooms. They moved their mouths, but he heard nothing but the sound of his wife's name.

"It is your wife, Carina."

Chapter 5

Jake watched Emery lift her luggage off the conveyor belt. Her fitted white shirt was slightly tucked into her gray jeans. Her long auburn hair was pulled into a ponytail, with wispy strands of gold surrounding her face, creating an angelic halo around her head.

Emery was checking inside one of her bags when she looked up and caught Jake's stare. Jake smiled and waved, hoping it wasn't too obvious that he was gawking.

"Good morning." Emery yawned as she rolled her luggage toward him.

"How was the flight? Did you get any sleep?"

"I couldn't sleep much." Emery yawned again, looking around the airport. "How about you?"

"Eh. Fair amount." Jake shrugged. He tried to avoid meeting Emery's eyes and looked up at the posters hung on the walls of the small baggage claim area. A bright poster of a smiling woman wearing a flower headdress had bold letters across the top—Feria de Las Flores.

"Hey, since we're here so early, do you want to check out the festival first?" he asked.

Emery tapped her lips with her pointer finger.

"Do you mind if we head straight to the hotel first? I have to do a little work before I will be able to enjoy myself here," she said.

"Sure."

"How about we check out the festival in the afternoon, okay?"

"Sounds good," he said with a twinkle in his eye. Jake followed Emery toward Customs, getting an eyeful of her perfect ass.

Keep it cool, Jake thought to himself.

***

Emery was wrapping up the final touches of a memo when the distant sound of beating drums and shouting trumpets piqued her curiosity. She pulled the sheer curtains away from the window. Hundreds of people gathered along the street below.

The crowd was smiling and cheering, all covered in glitter and face paint. Some people wore colorful feathers and others were adorned with beautiful headdresses made of flowers of every color. The swaying crowd looked like a living, breathing Monet painting.

The parade was full of flowers formed into large wreaths and propped on the backs of Colombian men. Chrysanthemums, roses, and carnations bounced along to the sound of the beating drums while dancers with bright garments weaved in between the wreaths.

Emery opened her luggage. Her formal dresses for the gala were wrapped in plastic and folded on top. She carefully grabbed the gowns out of the suitcase and hung them side by side on the door of the bathroom.

Traditionally, Emery preferred to wear her favorite black

dress for fancy events, but this time she had an unusual urge to wear something different. Something that stood out. She had found an exotic gown at the department store but didn't know if she would have the courage to wear it. She gazed at the fabric, admiring the sparkling gold sheath covered in intricate patterns of beaded rows that flowed like a river of luxury.

Emery twirled a strand of hair between her fingers, debating whether she should stick with her trusty black dress, or wear the flashy gold one with the plunging neckline. She forced herself to walk away for now and grabbed her favorite white tank top and a fresh pair of blue jeans.

When she reached Jake's hotel room, she hesitated. She recalled the way Jake was looking at her earlier at the airport. She was not blind to his attraction, but she needed to navigate it safely. She was his boss and friend. Nothing more.

Emery took a deep breath and lightly knocked on the door. A few moments later, Jake cracked it open. His cheeks were slightly flushed. His usually styled golden blond hair was damp.

"I just got out of the shower. I'll be ready in a couple of minutes," Jake said. He flashed her a bright smile and turned back to his room, leaving the door slightly ajar. Emery accidentally caught a glimpse of his glistening, muscular back, his hotel towel wrapped around his tapered waist.

"Take your time," she said as her eyes darted around the hotel hallway, trying to look anywhere but at the godlike half-naked body in the room in front of her.

Emery traced her lips with her fingertip as she tried thinking of anything but Jake getting dressed.

Jake came out in blue jeans and a gray fitted V-neck shirt.

It hugged his muscular chest tightly when he reached for his back pockets, checking for his wallet and his keys.

"You ready to go?" Emery blushed as she tucked a strand of hair behind her ear.

"You bet." Jake smiled and guided Emery toward the elevators, placing a hand on the small of her back.

Heat rose in her cheeks as they walked down the hall. She was relieved when Jake released his hand to touch the elevator button.

That didn't mean anything, right?

She looked up at Jake, who was patiently gazing at the digital sign above the elevator.

Ten … Eleven … Twelve …

He's a friend, she thought. Thirteen … Fourteen …

I'm his boss. Fifteen … Sixteen …

Bing.

The elevator doors opened, and Jake gestured for Emery to proceed. "Ladies first."

Emery and Jake stepped out onto the street, and their ears were filled with Latin music and the constant hum of strangers laughing and calling out into the warm afternoon air. Dancers with flowing yellow skirts shuffled back and forth, swaying the fabric from left to right. A marching band followed closely behind, shaking their maracas and beating leather-bound drums to a tribal beat.

The crowd clapped and yelled as the song came to an end. Another wave of dancers and musicians made their way into Emery's view. She watched as men on stilts towered over the sea of people. They waved and threw candy and flowers into the streets. One of the men on stilts caught Emery's eye and slowly made his stilted walk toward her. He bent at his hips to offer Emery a long-stemmed rose with hot-pink petals. She pressed her nose gently into the flower and breathed in.

"Gracias!" she shouted, waving as the stilted man gave her a wink before returning to the parade.

"Borojo, or limonada de coco?" Jake asked, holding two plastic cups in the air for Emery to choose.

Emery bit her bottom lip as she peered inside each drink. The limonada de coco was thick and creamy, garnished with coconut shavings. The other drink looked like a funky brown shake.

"What is 'borojo'?" Emery asked.

"According to the vendor, it's a fruit from the west side of the country." He had a playful look in his eye. He pursed his lips as if he were holding back from telling her something.

"And?"

Jake laughed and shook his head.

"What?" Emery laughed. "Tell me."

"It's considered a local aphrodisiac."

Emery rolled her eyes and gave him a playful shove.

"I'll be taking the limonada, thank you." Emery snatched the white drink from Jake's hand. She took a sip and welcomed the medley of sweet coconut and tangy citrus flavors.

"This is amazing!" Emery shouted over the crowd. "How's yours?"

Jake took a cautious sip of the brown mixture and immediately retched.

"Ugh!" He coughed and spat the rest of his sip back into the cup.

"Tastes like bad cheese," he said, wiping his mouth.

Emery giggled.

"Here, you try it." Jake raised the slop in Emery's direction.

"Uh, no," Emery said as she dodged away.

"Seriously, try it."

"Absolutely not! You said it tasted like bad cheese!" Emery laughed.

"Okay! I give up." Jake smiled and threw his cup in the trash, his hands up in surrender.

"Let's head over there. I want to see more of the city," Emery shouted.

They walked through the streets of Medellín, passing through hundreds of people watching the flower parade. Emery was falling in love with the vibrant city by the minute. She relished in the bright colors and playful music and pondered how different it was from home.

Emery felt a tingle at the back of her neck, and she looked to her side and caught Jake's stare. He had been watching her, and now that he was caught, he bashfully looked away.

"Hold up," Jake called to Emery as they approached a small brick building nestled between two tall office buildings. Emery looked at the sign in the front that read Solorzano.

"Do you mind if I stop in here for a minute?" Jake motioned with his thumb. "I think this is my tux shop."

Emery nodded and turned her gaze to the crowds of people dancing and laughing in the streets. "If you don't mind, I'm going to stay out here and watch the parade some more."

"I'll be right back."

As Jake walked into the shop, a tall man with broad shoulders and striking blue-green eyes walked out. Emery watched him curiously. He looked troubled, or deep in thought. He had a rugged look to him, a square jaw covered in dark stubble, and dust-covered jeans. He pulled out a cigarette, and Emery continued to watch him while sipping on her limonada de coco.

The man folded a receipt in his hand and shoved it in his pocket. Taking a drag of his cigarette, he looked up and locked on to Emery's gaze.

Crap! I'm staring. Embarrassed, she spun around to escape. She made less than a half step before she collided with a big, sweaty back. Limonada de coco splattered all over Emery's shirt and on the man in front of her.

Her drink soaked through her white tank top and into her bra. Emery gasped, struggling to breathe as the icy liquid touched her skin. The man turned around and cursed in Spanish. Catching her breath, Emery felt adrenaline rise into the back of her throat.

Emery looked back to see if the handsome stranger was still there, and she found him walking toward her.

Oh God. Panic arose as he approached.

***

The girl was soaking wet, her mouth agape. People in the crowd turned to look when the drenched man started shouting. He was drunk, gesturing wildly with his hands.

The woman muttered apologies. She sounded American. Although she looked calm, the man continued to wail in her face. Snickering and laughter grew with each insult the man sputtered out of his drunken mouth.

"You filthy whore! Why can't you look where you're going?"

Luca gritted his teeth and stomped on his cigarette with the heel of his boot. He coolly walked toward the spectacle, pushing away some of the men who swarmed the scene.

"Que pasa?" Luca said, inches from the drunk man's face.

Sweat dripped down the man's forehead and into his burly mustache. Black curly hair wrapped around the man's head like a half-eaten donut. His white shirt clung to his doughy body while he huffed about the clumsy girl in front of him.

"This stupid bitch wasn't looking where she was going."

"Take it easy. It was an accident. You don't have to talk to her like that."

"I can talk to her however I want. She's an idiot."

"Apologize, now," Luca said firmly, rolling up his sleeves one at a time. His heartbeat quickened. His hands balled into fists, and he waited for the short man to make a move.

Bystanders hooted and howled, egging the men on.

"Break his nose!"

"Punch his fat head!"

The crowd was growing wild.

A soft hand rested on Luca's arm. He looked down to find the freckled woman looking up through her thick lashes. "Thank you, but that's enough," the woman said. She took out her wallet and calmly handed the angry man a stack of pesos.

"Here, sir. This will be the last time I say it. I am sorry for spilling on you. Now please take this money and buy yourself a new shirt. It's the least I can do."

Luca and the fat man were dumbstruck by the quiet and collected demeanor of the young woman, unfazed by the degrading insults. Her posture remained tall and proud, like a queen dismissing her disciples.

The fat man took the money and grunted something under his breath before walking away. The crowd groaned disappointedly and turned back toward the festival streets for better entertainment.

Luca watched the woman relax, breathing heavily, her queen-like stature vanishing. He looked upon a demure young woman shaking in a soaked tank top, revealing a taupe-colored lace bra underneath.

"Are you okay?" Luca asked, looking over his shoulder to find a couple of snickering teenage boys. Luca raised his tuxedo bag to block their view and stepped in closer.

The young woman followed his gaze to her shirt, and her face immediately flushed a deep shade of scarlet as she folded her arms over her chest. She looked up at Luca and gave him an embarrassed smile. Then she did the most hypnotizing thing with her mouth, taking her bottom lip between her teeth. Her plump lips looked so sensual, so deliciously innocent. The breath escaped Luca's lips.

"I'm fine, thank you," she said.

The strands of hair around her face were dripping wet, and she had a splatter mark on her chin. Luca carefully raised his thumb to her face and wiped off the white goop.

The magnetic pull he felt when he touched her soft skin made him delirious with desire. He would have cupped her face with his hands and claimed her mouth right then and there if she hadn't looked away.

"Thank you for coming to my rescue, but I didn't need your help," she said.

"You made that pretty clear."

She smiled up at him.

"What were you doing running off like that?" Luca asked. "You looked like a conejita darting into oncoming traffic."

"A conejita?"

"Yes, a little rabbit."

He laughed at the memory of her slender frame bouncing off the man's fat back.

The young woman looked guilty under her thick lashes, but she smiled with her hands in the air as if she didn't know what he was talking about.

"Emery!" a man interrupted. "Is everything okay?"

Luca looked up. A blond-haired man quickly approached them. A tuxedo bag was draped over his shoulder. Luca recalled walking past him at the shop.

"Jake," she said, "I accidentally spilled my drink and—"

"Jesus Christ, you're practically naked," Jake said possessively, taking her under his arm. "And who are you?"

Luca looked at the couple. Emery and Jake, he had gathered. A tiny crack of disappointment ached in his heart.

"My name is Luca," he said, stepping back.

"I accidentally spilled my drink on a very drunk, very angry Colombian man. He was yelling at me, and Luca was kind enough to come over and help."

"It turns out she didn't need my help," Luca said, looking down at her. "She gracefully handled it by herself."

"Well, you helped give me a moment to think by distracting him."

"It was nothing."

Jake cleared his throat, irritated. "We better get going. It was nice to meet you, Luke."

"Luca."

"Right."

"You two have a great evening," Luca said as he watched Jake pull Emery away. The strings of his heart detached from the beautiful girl in another man's arms.

***

"You really need to be more careful. This place is full of snakes like that guy." Jake shook his head with disgust. "I shouldn't have let you wait on the street alone."

"Don't be so dramatic," Emery replied. "He was just trying to help."

"You need to be careful down here. You can't trust anyone. This is why we have to hold our negotiations at a secured office downtown. Even the coffee farmers can't be trusted."

Emery rolled her eyes.

"Don't you remember what happened two years ago?"

"What are you talking about?"

"One of the farmers literally strangled *your* predecessor during a meeting. It was a whole thing. The cops came and everything."

Emery shuddered.

"I'm just saying you need to be careful, that's all."

"Okay, Jake." She raised her hands to dismiss the conversation.

Emery chewed on her lower lip. She knew Jake was right, but she didn't like how he was patronizing her.

Jake watched her expression with a frown. "Hey, it's getting dark. Maybe we should head back and get ready for the gala?"

"Before we go, I just want one more thing," Emery said.

"And what's that?"

"Another limonado." She smiled playfully. "My tank top seems to have taken my drink."

Chapter 6

Fernando spent the morning spraying the fields with a pesticide. His lungs felt coated with the stuff, despite using the face mask his uncle bought him. He found himself coughing so violently that he was grateful to be back in the office, stacking papers on the desk instead.

His mind clouded with worry now that his father knew about Luisa. *My dad is going to kill me*, Fernando thought.

It wasn't Luisa's fault that her father accidentally killed Fernando's mother, but his father would never forgive the Santiagos. A week after Jose Santiago was convicted of manslaughter, Luisa had shown up at Fernando's front step. Tears had stained her blotchy cheeks, and she stood at their front doorstep unable to lift her head for the longest time. She was holding a basket of flowers and cookies in one hand, a letter in another.

Her hand shook when she gave Fernando the letter. She parted her lips, softly saying, "I am so sorry for your loss."

"Did you know my mother?" Fernando had asked.

She shook her head and wiped the tear off her cheek.

"Que pasa?" Fernando's father interjected, walking up behind Fernando. His eyes were bloodshot red and the stench of alcohol from the night before permeated the air. "Who are you?" he barked. He reached over to grab the letter and tore the envelope like an animal.

"I should go," Luisa said, her large brown eyes filled with sadness. That was the moment Fernando had fallen in love with her. He watched her dash to her bike, but before she could ride off, Fernando's father stomped down the steps.

"You! Diabla!" he shouted. "You can tell your father he can rot behind those bars or I will kill him the next chance I get. Never come here again!"

Tears streamed down the girl's face as she pushed the pedals up the rocky path.

"Papa! Que pasa?"

Fernando touched his father's shoulder who swung around and clubbed Fernando in the jaw. He keeled over in pain.

"La bruja is the daughter of your mother's murderer," Raphael snarled. He grabbed the basket and tossed it out onto the lawn. Flowers fell from the sky, and cookies settled into the dirt. He squeezed the letter in his fist before letting the crumpled paper fall to the ground. He stormed into the house and slammed the door shut.

Fernando hesitated before he reached for the letter and uncrumpled it. He read the words, and his heart broke again for his mother, and for the sad girl on the porch.

Dear Señor Mendoza,

Words cannot express how deeply sorry I am for what my father has done. Please accept my sincerest condolences for you and your family.

Sincerely,
Luisa Santiago

Perhaps it would have been easier if Fernando had been angry like his father, but instead, he felt a deep desire to console the girl. Just as he had lost his mother in the car accident, she had lost her father, who had been sentenced to jail for ten years.

Fernando tore open the schedule book on the desk, ripping the bottom corner completely off. He groaned at his mishap and found a piece of scotch tape to put the page back together.

On the schedule, a delivery was due for the Carmesi Restaurant. He leaped out of his chair before he could finish the rest of his office work. The stacks of paper found their way back into disarray in Fernando's flurry.

He bolted through the lot and into the small warehouse on the plantation, opening the door to find Señor Garcia tending to the roaster. The roasting coffee in the air agitated his lungs.

"Buenos días, Fernando," Señor Garcia said over Fernando's coughing.

"Buenos días, Señor Garcia," Fernando finally spat out. "I was going to head into town. I can make the local deliveries today if you'd like."

"Sí, por favor. I have a lot of work to do here," Señor Garcia said, nodding to the large bags of coffee sitting in the corner.

"Do you mind if I use your truck?" Fernando asked.

"Claro."

***

Luisa stood just behind the restaurant window, talking to an older couple sitting at a booth. She was wearing her black button-up dress and a white apron wrapped around her waist. Her hair was braided and rested midway down her back.

A tiny bell rang as Fernando stepped through the restaurant

door, and Luisa looked up to find Fernando smiling at her from across the room. He gestured toward his box of coffee and walked behind the cash register desk and down the hall to find Señor Rojas, the restaurant manager, taking inventory in their stockroom.

"Fernando!" Señor Rojas said. "I wasn't expecting to see you today."

"Ah, sí. I am helping out Señor Garcia."

Fernando placed the cardboard box of coffee on the counter as Señor Rojas scribbled on his checkbook. Fernando nervously tapped his fingers on the table.

Señor Rojas looked up from his checkbook. "In a hurry?"

"Perdón."

Señor Rojas slowly tore off the check and placed it on the table.

"Gracias!" Fernando said quickly, exchanging the check for the receipt. He dashed out of the stockroom and thundered down the hallway.

Luisa appeared from the kitchen. "Fernando," she whispered. "Come here."

Luisa led him into a small break room across the kitchen. She closed the door. A small square-shaped plastic table and two chairs were placed across from a miniature fridge. The ceiling light dangled precariously from the wall and flickered on and off.

"Luisa," Fernando started.

"Shh," Luisa silenced him.

She looked up with her big brown eyes and cupped his face with her hands, a glint of playfulness in the corner of her mouth. She licked her bottom lip.

Fernando let out a whimper as the rush of his arousal

scorched through his body.

She leaned in for a kiss when Fernando put his hands on her shoulders to stop her.

"Luisa. My father knows."

"Qué?" she gasped.

"I have no idea what to do. He left for Medellín, but he'll be back in a couple of days. I am really worried about what he might do when he gets back."

"He won't hurt you," she said tenderly, caressing his hair. "I won't let him."

Fernando leaned into her hands.

"It's going to be okay. You'll see. Maybe it's a good thing he'll be gone for a couple of days. He'll have some time to get used to the idea so he can be more rational."

Fernando nodded and looked down at her worried face. He wanted to believe that his father could be rational about anything. He just hadn't proved he could.

He cupped her chin and tilted it up to see her straight on.

"You are so beautiful, mi amor," he said.

Luisa's cheeks flushed the sweetest shade of pink. She tried to look away, but he cupped her chin lightly, holding her gaze. He couldn't wait any longer and claimed her mouth with his, carefully sucking on her bottom lip, which had been wet and ready for him. Luisa kissed him back, letting her tongue lightly caress his in return. She pulled him closer and firmly pressed her hands against his back.

Fernando breathed in her sweet scent. His hands became wild with desire, and he reached around her waist to bring her closer. He wanted to feel every millimeter of her body through her dress. He pressed her back against the wall. Luisa's breath caught in her throat as he sucked on the base of her neck. His hands traveled up the soft middle of her slender thighs.

"Luisa. Your break is over!" Señor Rojas called from behind the door.

Fernando and Luisa froze in terror.

"Coming!" Luisa called back, releasing Fernando. She smoothed out her dress while hushing Fernando.

"How do I look?" she asked worriedly.

Her lips were swollen, and some of the hair had come out of her braid.

Fernando shrugged. "As beautiful as ever," he whispered before giving her a kiss on the cheek.

"I have to go," she said, looking up at him through her thick, dark lashes. "I'll see you tomorrow?"

Fernando gave her a smile and kissed her forehead.

"Tomorrow," he whispered as she walked out of the room. She looked both ways to ensure no one was around.

"Don't worry about your father. It's all going to work out."

Chapter 7

Raphael parked his truck and stepped out onto the city street. A stampede of drunk festivalgoers swarmed him. Sounds of drum music, shouts, and laughter filled the air and confetti tickled his face. The festival was in full bloom.

What a pain in the ass. He needed to find his brother in the midst of the chaos, and he had no idea where to start.

He plowed through the sea of happy patrons in search of Luca. The more steps he took into the city, the more flower petals and confetti piled on top of him. Raphael attempted to bat away the streamers that covered his face. He looked around the tall buildings and recognized the doorway of the Coffee Benz office. Picking up his pace, his walk evolved into a light jog. A colorful rainbow of paper streamers flowed in the wind behind him.

He reached for the door handle and tugged. The door didn't budge.

Raphael scratched his head, wondering where Luca could be. He yanked out a few feathers from his hair and dropped them to the ground. The wind picked them up and carried them into the air. As he watched the feathers fly away, he caught sight of the motel sign down the street. Hope filled his chest, and he rushed to the motel.

A portly middle-aged woman behind the counter giggled at the sight of him, covered in an array of colors and sparkles. Raphael clenched his fists as he approached the chuckling woman.

"Is Luca Mendoza staying at this hotel?"

"Un momento," she said, stifling her giggle. Raphael watched as the receptionist clubbed her thick fingers onto the keyboard. The clicking sounds pounded all the way to Raphael's temples.

"Well?" Raphael asked. His nostrils flared.

After a few moments of silence, the woman finally responded.

"Si, señor," she replied without removing her gaze from the computer screen. "Would you like me to phone him?"

"Por favor."

The woman punched a few numbers on the desk phone and carefully handed the handset to Raphael.

With every passing ring, Raphael sent daggers through his eyes at the receptionist. Her cheerful demeanor melted away.

"Would you like me to leave a message for him?"

"No."

Raphael turned to leave and caught his reflection in the mirror. He paused at the sight. His face was covered in bright shades of chalk powder and glitter. He had streamers intertwined and tangled all around him. He looked ridiculous.

He vigorously rubbed his face and brushed off his clothes before heading out of the motel, leaving the dumbfounded receptionist behind him.

At least he knew where Luca was staying tonight. This meant he could take a break from searching and head over to the bar for a drink, or two. He crossed the street to the tavern on the corner.

"What can I get you?" the bartender asked.

"Guaro," Raphael said.

A group of men walked through the door, bringing along a cloud of heavy cigar smoke and the smell of stale liquor. Raphael recognized a few of the men from their coffee farmers' association and smiled. "Que pasa?" Raphael stood with open arms, giving a few of them strong embraces.

"Are you all here to see Emerson Smith too?" Raphael asked.

The men nodded in defeat.

"We've got to do something!" Raphael shouted, pounding his fist on the bar. The men cheered in response.

The bartender cautiously put the guaro in front of Raphael.

"But first, to us!" Raphael raised his glass in the air. "To the hardworking coffee farmers who deserve better. May we show this gringo just who he is messing with."

Several rounds of shots later, Raphael leaned his body against the bar and wrapped one arm around Carlos to prevent himself from falling.

"And that sick son-of-bitch couldn't look me in the eye while I asked him how we were going to afford the fertilizer he was mandating," Raphael slurred. The men sat around Raphael and Carlos as if it were story time in a preschool classroom.

"I told him." Raphael nodded and looked at his fellow farmers. "I said to the man, I'll go ahead and take my shits around the whole plantation from now on!"

The circle of men erupted in laughter.

"How's that for saving the company some money?"

"Where do you think those greedy sons of bitches are tonight?" Carlos asked.

"Raping and pillaging what's left of our businesses," Raphael muttered sarcastically as he took another sip of his drink.

"Sleeping with your wife, Carlos!" yelled a man in the back. Another round of laughter burst from the group of men. All but Raphael, whose face grew long, and his eyes went dark.

The bartender leaned over the bar and beckoned for Raphael and Carlos to come closer.

"I heard there was a gala tonight," he whispered.

"What gala?" Raphael straightened and leaned close to the bartender's face.

"The Coffee Farmers Association gala," The bartender paused to look around. "I assumed you—"

"You assumed we would be invited," Carlos interrupted.

Raphael shook his head in disgust. "Of course those filthy rich, greedy pieces of shit are having a fancy expensive gala the night before they squeeze every penny out of us," he spat.

The men shouted in protest, their voices stacking on top of each other. It was impossible to hear anything in the entire bar. The men pounded their fists on the table and cussed at the top of their lungs.

Raphael scratched his scruffy chin. Was his brother attending the gala without him? What kind of operation was he running? Whose side was he on? The heat from Raphael's pumping heart crept into his jaw, and his teeth clenched in fury.

"Listen up!" Raphael yelled over the belligerent farmers, and they silenced almost immediately.

"We're going to make this right. They can't treat us like cattle anymore. I'm heading over there to give that bastard, Emerson Smith, a piece of my mind. Who's with me?"

The bar cheered and whistled. Raphael grabbed an unclaimed shot glass of guaro and took a drink.

He wiped his mouth with the back of his wrist and looked at the crowd. "Let's do this."

Chapter 8

As Luca was putting on his tuxedo, he couldn't keep his mind off the woman he'd met in front of the tux shop. He chuckled at the memory of how easily embarrassed she got when their eyes first met. She looked so young and helpless, but she handled the angry fat man with grace and maturity. *She was a beautiful, walking contradiction.* He smiled. But his smile quickly faded when he thought of the Ken Barbie doll that strolled in and took her under his arm. If Jake was her type, then she and Luca would never have worked out anyway.

Luca raised an eyebrow at his reflection in the motel mirror. His cheap tuxedo rental didn't look bad, even with his bow tie lying loosely around his neck. His hair was gelled back, and his face was cleanly shaven. No stubble in sight.

You have more important things to think about. The family is depending on you tonight.

Luca stopped his train of thought to concentrate on his bow tie. He struggled with the flimsy piece of fabric and couldn't seem to get the tie to follow his will.

"Dammit," he spat, giving up and letting the tie drape around his neck like a limp worm. Luca tried one more time to tie his bow and then threw his hands up.

"You win," he scoffed and left the motel room in defeat.

Luca walked down the street toward the Hotel du Park Royal. The early evening air felt cool against his heated skin. He needed to find someone to help him with his tie, but more importantly, he needed to figure out a way inside the gala.

As he walked into the front doors of the hotel entrance, Luca noticed a line of couples in formal attire in front of the grand ballroom. Women were dressed in full-length ball gowns and giant, glittering necklaces. The men wore the finest tuxedos and fanciest shoes he had ever seen. A few of them were carrying a small rectangular slip of paper, and Luca's eyes darted to the front of the line, where the gala receptionist and her guard were accepting invitations.

Shit.

He walked closer to see who was accepting the invitations. A young woman was dressed in a tight-fitting black dress with dangerously high heels. She had a giant peacock feather hair clip behind her right ear, and the eyeshadow to match.

Luca watched the saucy receptionist take each of the couples' invitations while the security guard oversaw the intake of people.

Luca got in line, and nervously played with his bow tie straps. His heart thumped inside his cheap, rental tuxedo, and his palms began to sweat.

He was next.

Luca's nerves almost made him keel over when he realized that the receptionist was looking directly at him.

"Buenos noches, señorita." Luca smiled bashfully, flashing his set of dimples. "I was hoping that you could help me."

The receptionist batted her eyes playfully. "What can I do for you, handsome?" she asked, leaning at the edge of her seat.

"I'm in a little bit of trouble, you see. I can't seem to get along with this tie." Luca lifted either side of his untied bow tie around his neck and pleaded with his eyes.

"You poor thing. Of course I can help. Let me come around."

She leaned forward out of her chair, bending just enough to give Luca a full demonstration of her cleavage. Locking her eyes on Luca, she sauntered around the corner of the table but miscalculated and slammed into the table corner.

"Ow!" She winced in pain, but immediately flipped her hair back to regain her composure. Her hair was now entangled with her peacock feather, and she ungracefully limped toward Luca.

"Are you okay, señorita?" Luca asked.

"Sí," she said as she grabbed on to his tie, pulling his neck down. "Come closer, honey." She worked on his tie while Luca fought the urge to look down her dress.

"I take it your wife was unable to help you with your tie this evening?"

"I'm not married." Luca smiled.

"I see." She smiled back, stepping away from Luca and admiring her work. "There you go, handsome," she purred.

Her hair was still in complete disarray, and she limped back toward the table. She bent over to reach for a pen, and her short dress moved up her legs, giving Luca a glimpse of the tiny crease below her butt cheeks.

My God, woman. Luca's cheeks flushed as he tried to look away. The security guard had his eyes planted on the receptionist's ass.

Luca's heart pounded as she approached him. He froze as he waited for her to ask him for his invitation. Instead, the receptionist limped back over to Luca and took his hand. With her pen, she scribbled a few numbers on his palm.

"Save me a dance." The receptionist winked before limping the rest of the way to her chair behind the registration table.

Luca looked down to find her phone number sitting inside a drawn heart on his hand. He gulped and walked toward the entrance of the ballroom. When he looked back, the receptionist playfully chewed on the tip of her pen and batted her eyes.

Relief washed over Luca. His blood pressure normalized as he walked through the entrance of the grand ballroom.

Large glittering chandeliers hung from the ceiling. Massive candelabras stood in the center of each table, with white lilies and an array of sparkling crystal beads that twinkled with each passing step.

An Afro-Colombian jazz orchestra filled the room with vibrant music. There were men and women dancing on the tiled dance floor. Luca looked around to find expensive plates of caviar and shrimp cocktail on the banquet tables. Servers with trays of champagne buzzed from table to table, pollinating the people with sparkling conversation starters.

These sons of bitches.

While he was fighting to save his plantation, these greedy businessmen were living a life of luxury. He continued to survey the high-class society and realized he felt as out of place as the receptionist lady looked.

He swallowed the sour taste of disgust and prowled through the crowd in search of his target: Emerson Smith.

***

Emery walked into the hotel room to find both gala dresses

hanging up on the bathroom door. After such a colorful day at the festival, the plain black dress just didn't feel right anymore. She reached for the black dress and tossed it back in her suitcase.

Gazing at the gold dress, Emery felt a surge of adrenaline. Was she really going to go out in public in that?

She slipped into the gown. It hugged her curves perfectly and flowed down to her glittering stilettos. The plunging neckline came together just below her breastbone, exposing just enough cleavage to put her out of her comfort zone.

I can do this.

Emery stepped out of the elevator. The main lobby buzzed with Colombia's elite socialites. Emery stopped in front of the tall mirror to inspect her look. Her hair was pulled back in a low chignon, with loose long curls draped on either side of her face. Topaz chandelier earrings caught the light from the sun peeking through the window, creating a playful pattern around her shoulders.

Just as she lost the courage to walk any farther into the lobby, a familiar voice came from behind her.

"Emery? Is that you?"

Jake stared at Emery with his mouth agape. His eyes trailed the length of her dress, and he shook his head in disbelief.

"Good heavens, Emery," Jake said. "I can't even … I don't even know what to say."

Emery's cheeks flared, and she looked down at her stilettos.

"Is it too much?" she asked bashfully.

"You're gorgeous," he said. "Is that weird that I said that?"

"Maybe a little. But thank you."

Jake's sun-kissed skin was a handsome, stark contrast to the velvety black Armani tuxedo. His blond hair was slicked back, and he smelled of a spicy aftershave.

"You clean up well yourself." Emery smiled.

Jake lifted his elbow to escort her to the gala. A wave of heat crept up her neck as she slipped her hand around Jake's muscular arm and allowed him to lead her into the grand ballroom.

Emery took in the beautiful grand ballroom decor. It was clear the association spared no expense for the event. She felt a pang of guilt in her chest as she picked up a champagne flute from a server's silver platter. It didn't feel right to be celebrating in such luxury when the company was in financial trouble.

Suddenly, a sharp impact of a shoulder bumping into her back knocked her off balance. She lost her grip on Jake and almost toppled forward.

"Lo siento!" a man said. "I am so sorry."

Emery turned toward the assailant and was met with the biggest, apologetic bright blue eyes.

Wait a minute, she thought. *I recognize those eyes.*

The color drained from the man's face. "Emery." Luca swallowed. "Dios mio."

A flutter came from deep in her stomach as she realized she was looking at the man she had met on the street. The ruggedly handsome man had swapped his blue jeans and cowboy boots for a sleek black tuxedo. The stubble on his face was gone, and his hair was combed back. The dimples in his smile sent shivers down Emery's spine.

"Emery, are you all right?" Jake reached for her, putting his hands on her shoulders.

"I'm fine," Emery said. "Look who's here. Our friend from the tux shop." She gestured toward Luca.

"Again, I am so sorry for bumping into you," Luca said. "At least I didn't have limonada de coco in my hands."

Luca winked at Jake and turned back to Emery.

"You look stunning, Emery," Luca said before turning to Jake to shake his hand. "Nice to see you again too, Yake."

"It's Jake," he corrected irritably. Jake wrapped his arm around her shoulder.

Every muscle in her upper body contracted.

"So are you in the coffee business, or are you working at this party?" Jake asked.

"I own a coffee plantation," Luca answered, but his gaze fixated on Emery.

"Oh, I see. You're a coffee farmer." Jake smiled.

Emery needed to get out of Jake's clutches, especially when she knew he was trying to belittle Luca in front of her. Emery downed her champagne glass and immediately reached toward the nearest waiter, unleashing herself from Jake's arm.

"More champagne, anyone?" Emery's voice cracked.

"Allow me," Luca said, grabbing two flutes from the tray and offering one to both Emery and Jake.

Emery gratefully accepted it and downed the glass.

Jake and Luca watched her in amusement. As she finished the champagne, she quickly grabbed the other one in Luca's hand.

"Thank you," Emery said, tilting her head back again.

"Jake!" a distant voice shouted from the crowd. An older gentleman waved for Jake to join their group. He was a frail man with thin-rimmed glasses that sat crookedly across his face. His pale complexion and balding hairline made him look much older than he was. Emery recognized him as the vice president of the Medellín office.

Jake seemed to hesitate, eyeing both Emery and Luca.

"Will you be okay?" Jake asked.

"Of course. Go on." Emery ushered him.

"Please excuse me." Jake gave a slight bow to Luca and walked to the circle of men engaged in what looked like a confidential conversation.

Perhaps they didn't recognize me, she thought. She waited for Jake to beckon her over, but he never turned around.

"I take it your boyfriend works with those men?" Luca asked, breaking the silence between them.

Emery was taking a sip of another champagne flute and nearly inhaled it.

"Boyfriend?" she spat through her cough, gasping for air.

Luca placed a concerned hand on Emery's back, where the dress mirrored the plunging neckline. His warm and gentle touch sent electric currents up Emery's neck.

"Sorry." She coughed again, holding up one finger while she took another sip of her champagne to calm her throat. "Jake is not my boyfriend."

She watched Luca raise his eyebrows in surprise.

"No?" he asked with palpable doubt.

"No," she started to say as she turned her head toward Jake, who was still conversing with the vice president without her.

"Jake works for me."

Luca choked on his champagne, coughing up the bubbles.

Emery giggled while Luca tried calming his throat with more champagne.

"Are you going to copy every embarrassing thing I've done today?" Emery playfully laughed.

"It appears that way." Luca laughed at himself. "So he works for you, really?"

"Yes." Emery smiled wide.

"Then why does he act like he owns you?"

"What do you mean? He does not," Emery scoffed. She bit her lip, remembering all the times he put his arm around her shoulders, especially in front of Luca.

As if Luca could read her mind, he nodded. "You see it now? He treats you like you are a toy he doesn't want to share."

"He's been a work friend of mine for years. He's protective, but it's because we're friends."

Luca raised an eyebrow and visibly decided to drop the subject.

"Would you care for a dance?" Luca offered his hand.

"I can't dance, unfortunately. I've got two left feet."

"What do you mean you have two left feet? They look normal to me," Luca said, looking down at her shoes.

"I didn't mean that literally." Emery laughed. "I just mean I don't know how to dance."

"Ah. Well then, you are very lucky tonight. Because I can teach you."

"You'll regret it if you try," Emery pleaded.

"You'll regret it if you don't," Luca said, flashing the crescent moons alongside his handsome smile.

She found herself being led toward the dance floor. Panic settled in.

"Follow my lead," Luca said, placing one hand at the small of her back, bringing her in close.

She could barely hear the music over the sound of blood pumping in her ears. The champagne had given her just enough courage not to throw up all over the dance floor.

Luca swayed his hips in step with the beat, but Emery was a stick in mud. She tried taking her first step, but her stiletto heel landed on Luca's toe.

"Ow!" Luca winced.

"I am so sorry. Really. I told you I can't dance."

Luca smiled and hugged her in closer.

"Don't think about it. Just trust me."

Emery moved with the swaying of Luca's hips. She didn't even have to take a step. He was able to carry her along with the beat, rocking her from left to right. It felt like she was flying.

Emery relaxed into his hold while he hummed the melody of the tune in her ear. She breathed in his intoxicating scent and got lost in the feeling of weightlessness.

When the rhythm picked up, she was able to follow the sway of Luca's hips. Just as she was getting the hang of dancing, Luca twirled her around and went for the dip. Emery didn't know what to do with her limbs and her knee shot up, making direct contact with Luca's groin.

"Ay!" Luca groaned, propping her back up. He keeled over in pain.

"Oh my God, Luca!" Emery cried, putting her hands on his back to comfort him. "I am so sorry!"

"I'm fine," Luca said breathlessly. He winced as they shuffled off the dance floor.

"Luca, I feel terrible. I told you I couldn't dance."

Luca started to catch his breath, and he stood up straight.

"It's okay." He laughed. "You were right. You really can't dance."

Emery playfully hit him on the shoulder and crossed her arms. Her lower lip pouted in protest.

"I'm just teasing you. Thank you for the dance," he said, fully composed now.

"That's funny. It sounded like you said 'thank you for the dance,' but I think you actually meant 'thank you for kneeing me in the testicles.'"

Luca laughed so hard a tear pricked the corner of his eye.

"My dear Emery, you are absolutely enchanting."

"*Enchanting?*"Emery burst into laughter.

"What's so funny?"

"It's just not a very common way I've heard people describe me," she said as she blotted the tears of laughter from her eyes.

"How do people normally describe you?"

Emery thought pensively for a brief moment and flashed Luca a flirtatious smile. "Boring, predictable," she started to list, "controlling."

"No," Luca said, "there is *nothing* boring about you. Care for another drink?" he asked.

"Yes, please," Emery replied gratefully, as she was feeling the courage from her champagne start to wear off.

"I'll be right back," Luca promised. He grasped her right hand and raised it slowly toward his mouth, locking his blue-green eyes with hers. He gently kissed the tops of her knuckles, sending another electric charge from her hand up her arm.

Emery watched Luca walk toward the bar. As the tingles from his kiss still lingered on her hand, she shook her head in disbelief.

What is happening? She lightly patted her cheeks with her palms to compose herself.

"Where did *Casablanca* go?" Jake interrupted her thoughts as he offered Emery a new glass of champagne.

"*Luca,*"she corrected him, "was just getting us another round of champagne."

Jake looked past Emery toward the bar and smirked.

"For you or for her?"

Emery turned to follow Jake's gaze. She spotted Luca leaning over the bar, talking to a young woman wearing a ridiculously short black dress and a large feather in her hair. The woman wrapped her arms around his neck and twirled the hair on the back of Luca's head.

Emery's stomach plummeted.

"Looks like Luca is a busy man," Jake said.

Emery stared at the woman, who was laughing at something Luca said. Luca leaned in to whisper in the woman's ear. Emery decided she'd had enough and turned to Jake. "So what did Mr. Bosworth have to say?"

Jake looked down at his shoes, and then out into the crowd as if he were trying to recall his conversation. "Ah, he was just asking about our plans for the week," Jake said, taking a sip of his own drink. "And he wanted to see if I wanted to play a round of golf while I was here."

Emery chewed on that for a moment, disappointed she wasn't included in the conversation, or the invitation to play golf as well. She didn't know how to play, but she would learn if she had been invited. It wasn't rare that Emery found herself on the outside of the good ol' boy network. She couldn't help but feel like she was purposefully being left out.

"Did he say anything about the negotiations this week? Will he be in attendance?" Emery looked Jake straight in the eye.

"Uh, no. But he did mention something about our quality rating. Apparently, we've been missing targets. I'll fill you in later."

Emery rolled her eyes and looked across the room toward Luca. The bartender had just set down two flutes of champagne in front of him, and he stood up. The woman in the short dress released her hand from his chest while he turned around. When he looked up, he locked eyes with Emery's icy stare.

Chapter 9

Emery tried to ignore the pang of jealousy that stirred her insides.

"Looks like *Loverboy* is on his way back," Jake said.

Luca approached cautiously and offered Emery a flute of champagne.

"Thank you," she said, taking a sip, trying to act like she wasn't jealous of the woman in the short dress. The bubbles buzzed around in her head, blocking out the inner voice telling her to slow down.

"Who's your lady friend over there?" Jake teased.

"The woman at the bar? She's nobody," Luca said directly to Emery, even though she didn't ask.

Emery smiled politely but quickly resumed looking out into the crowd.

"She certainly didn't look like nobody," Jake prodded. "It looked like she had a thing for you, pal. Maybe she didn't know you were a farmer."

Emery whipped around to give Jake an admonishing glare.

"So if I had told her I was a farmer, she would have left me alone? I wish I had thought of that," Luca quipped.

"Jake," Emery said, gritting her teeth.

"I'm just teasing him!" Jake threw his hands in the air. "Luca knows that he could get any girl he wants, even if he is just a farmer," Jake said.

"Jake!" Emery snapped.

"It's all right, Emery. Yake can tease all he wants," Luca said, proudly folding his arms. The confident look in his grin only seemed to irritate Jake more.

A tap on her shoulder broke Emery from her fiery gaze. "Emery?"

She turned to find a tall woman wearing a full-length green gown. She had soft wrinkles at the corners of her eyes, and lipstick that bled into the tiny creases around her mouth.

"Pardon me for the interruption. Can you be ready in about fifteen minutes?" she asked softly.

Emery nodded.

"Wonderful," she said, clasping her hands. "In the meantime, do you mind if I steal Jake for a moment? There was something our logistics manager wanted to run by him."

Emery looked up at Jake, who had been studying Luca behind his champagne glass.

"Jake. You are being beckoned again." Emery tilted her head to the woman in green, who was ushering him to follow her.

"Are you okay if I leave you alone again?" Jake asked.

"I'm fine," Emery reassured him. "Go ahead."

Jake hesitated again. "Just come get me if you need anything," he said as he looked back at Luca. "*Anything.*"

Emery nodded and shooed Jake away as she caught a glimpse of the logistics manager and his buddies eagerly waiting for Jake to approach them.

"I know it's none of my business, but does it bother you that Jake is getting pulled into all these business discussions without you?" Luca asked.

Emery shrugged. She tried appearing aloof by plastering a wide smile on her face.

"It doesn't bother me. If something important enough surfaces, then I will get involved."

Luca looked her over inquisitively, studying her facial expression with care.

"Come with me." Luca offered his arm to her.

Emery cautiously looked at his arm. Over her shoulder, she found Jake shaking hands with the men who circled around him.

"Don't worry, conejita. You can trust me," he said with a warm smile. He leaned down toward her ear and whispered gently, "There is something I want to show you."

They walked up the staircase onto one of the balconies overlooking the crowded ballroom. Behind them was a giant glass window along the back wall. Luca led her to it, and together they stared at the gold and pink hues of the sunset behind the city landscape.

"Wow," Emery said under her breath.

"It is beautiful, no?" Luca asked.

"Very."

"Almost as pretty as the woman standing by my side."

Emery looked at Luca quizzically. "Aren't you a charmer."

"'Charmer'? What is this meaning in English?"

"A flirt," she jabbed.

Luca was thoughtful for a minute. "Maybe so, but I'm only speaking the truth."

"So what's the deal with the woman downstairs?"

"What about her?"

"It seemed like you might have charmed her too."

"Not any more than you have charmed Jake."

"What are you talking about?"

Luca studied her face. "You really don't know?" He started to laugh.

"Don't you dare turn this around on me. Were you flirting with her too?"

Luca's laugh sobered, and he let out a sigh. He turned his gaze toward his shoes and looked up through his thick lashes.

"When I talk to women, sometimes they jump to the wrong conclusions." He shrugged and lifted his face so that he could look at her directly.

Emery cocked her brow and crossed her arms.

Luca placed his gentle hands on her shoulders and nudged her to face him.

"Emery. Listen to me. The woman at the bar helped me with my bow tie before I walked into the party. That's all. She might have thought I was making a pass at her, but I wasn't. I swear."

Emery looked down at her hands. How could she have felt so much jealousy toward that woman so quickly? She had only just met him. Emery shrugged off her insecurity and uncrossed her arms.

"Well, for the record, I have not flirted with Jake, nor have I charmed him. He's just being an overprotective friend."

"That's settled then. Now that we've moved on, let's celebrate. Care for another drink?" Luca asked, eyeing her empty glass.

***

Luca walked toward the staircase, smiling to himself. The thought of Emery crossing her arms in a pout was adorable and perplexing. How could a beautiful woman like her be so insecure and untrusting?

As he looked around the room, he still had no idea how to find Emerson Smith. Perhaps he could ask some people by the bar while he got another round of champagne.

Before he made his first step onto the stairs, a dark figure appeared on the first floor in a cowboy hat and flannel shirt. He looked out of place in the formal ballroom, and it was causing a stir among the crowd. *This guy better not be trouble.*

Luca watched the man stumble his way toward the staircase and grabbed the railing to keep him from swaying into nearby people. When he looked up, the familiar outline of his brother's face came into view. The pit of Luca's stomach began to curdle. While Luca scuffled down the flight of stairs to catch his brother, several other inebriated men staggered into the ballroom from the main entrance.

Raphael waved for the group of men to follow him.

Oh great, Luca thought to himself. *Raphael, the god of chaos, has a group of disciples.*

Luca met Raphael at the base of the stairs. He tucked his hand under Raphael's arm, and with a firm grip, Luca led him behind the staircase.

"Let go of me," Raphael hissed. His boozy breath invaded Luca's nostrils.

Luca tightened his grip, and Raphael winced in pain before whipping his arm out of Luca's grasp.

Luca looked around quickly, fighting the urge to clobber his brother in front of the entire gala. His heart pounded in his chest.

"Raphael," Luca said with a clenched jaw. "What are you doing here?"

Raphael attempted to smooth his wrinkled shirt with drunken pride. "I'm here to give Señor Emerson a piece of my mind."

Luca took a deep inhale to calm himself down. "I've got this taken care of. You need to leave. Now."

"How do I know what you're up to?" Raphael asked, raising his voice louder. "Huh? little brother?"

Luca raised his hands, motioning for Raphael to keep his voice down. "You're being ridiculous," he whispered back. "Go *home*, Raphael."

Raphael curled his lip with contempt.

"Look at you," he said, eyeing Luca's formal attire. "Just look at you in your fancy clothes and your fancy hair."

Raphael's entourage gathered around. They watched with hungry eyes as Raphael continued to rant.

"You're a traitor!" Raphael raised a hand in Luca's direction and let it flop down to his side. "You could be selling us out, for all I know! How do I trust you're not going to blow it like you did last time?"

Pressure wrapped around the crown of Luca's head. His temples throbbed. The fact that Raphael would even think about blaming Luca for the last round of negotiations was an absolute knife to the heart. After everything that Luca had done to pick up the pieces of Raphael's episode, Raphael was blaming *him? Will this ever end? Will I always be cleaning up the messes he makes?*

"Leave, or I will have the police escort you out!"

"No, mi hermano," Rafael said. "Get out of my way."

Before Luca could grab Raphael, the pack of drunken strays stepped forward, creating a protective barrier between Luca and their fearless leader.

Raphael walked through the crowd. One of the men patted Raphael's back, and Luca caught the glint of a curved wooden gun handle poking out from the man's belt.

Suddenly a new thought ran through his mind. *Emery.* If he couldn't stop his brother and the angry mob, then he needed to get her out of here. Luca bounded up the flight of stairs. His chest heaved, fighting for air as he reached Emery.

"Hey! Did you forget something?" Emery asked playfully as she placed a perfectly manicured hand on her hip.

Luca's mouth went dry, and he struggled to normalize his breath. "This is not a safe place for you anymore," he said, grabbing her hand to lead her down the stairs.

Emery pulled her hand back. "Where do you think you're taking me?"

"I can take you back to your hotel room."

"What?"

"I mean, I can take you anywhere else but here," he said.

"I can't leave with you now," Emery replied.

He placed his hands on Emery's shoulders. Her skin was soft, and her delicate frame screamed for protection. He had to get her out of there.

"Emery—"

"There you are," a familiar masculine voice interrupted. "I've been looking all over for you! They're ready for us. We need to go now," Jake said, holding out his hand, completely ignoring Luca.

"Actually, Emery was just leaving."

"Absolutely not, Casanova. She's coming with me."

Emery gave Luca a long, troubled stare before she brushed past him.

"Emery, please," he said to the back of her head. "You need

to leave."

***

Luca leaned over the balcony in search of the angry mob. He had lost sight of Raphael.

"Attencion," the woman in the green gown spoke into the microphone on stage in front of the band, who had quieted their instruments.

"Attention," she repeated in English. "Good evening, ladies and gentlemen."

Luca leaned on the balcony railing, his hands in his hair. He didn't know if he should run after Emery and throw her over his shoulder, or if he should call the police on his brother.

"I would now like to present to you our guests of honor this evening." The woman shifted the microphone into one hand and lifted her free hand in the direction of the crowd. "All the way from Coffee Benz Company world headquarters in Chicago, Illinois, please help me give a very warm welcome to Emerson Smith and Jake Whitmore!"

The ballroom erupted with applause.

Luca anxiously followed the direction of the woman's hand. Emery's sparkling dress floated through the sea of black tuxedos and long ball gowns. She was being escorted to the stage with Jake by her side.

Emery is Emerson Smith? Luca stood in stunned silence.

Emery accepted the microphone from the thin woman and raised it to her lips.

"Gracias," she spoke to the crowd. "Thank you."

Luca couldn't hear the words of Emery's speech, as he was frantically searching the ballroom for any trace of Raphael and his clan. If his brother was still there, Luca was sure that Emery was in danger now.

Luca caught a glimpse of their shadows toward the back of the ballroom. He raced down the flight of stairs and shouldered his way to the edge of the stage just as Emery and Jake were walking down the steps. The band played an upbeat tune, and the music blasted through the stage speakers.

"Emery!" Luca shouted over the beating drums. Her attention was turned to the crowd, and she waved as she was being helped off of the stage. He was getting closer, but she couldn't hear him.

Before he could approach her, a pair of strong hands stopped him.

"Luca, back off, okay?" Jake said.

"You need to get Emery out of here now."

"Oh yeah?" Jake said. "And why is that?"

Luca took a deep breath. "She's in danger."

"Yeah right," Jake brushed him off. "Back off, Zorro. I've got this. As long as she's with me, she'll be fine."

"This isn't a joke!"

"What's going on?" Emery asked.

Luca peered behind Jake's broad shoulders to find Emery standing with wide eyes.

"Emery. Please. You need to get out of here," Luca pleaded. He tried to maneuver around Jake, but Jake held him back.

"He's just trying to scare you into sleeping with him. It's the oldest trick in the book." Jake shoved Luca back a second time.

Luca tried to compose his temper.

"Emery," Luca begged.

"Come on, Emery, let's find Mr. Bosworth. He's been wanting to talk to you," Jake said, knocking his shoulder into

Luca. Emery looked back at Luca, concern growing on her face.

Luca ground his teeth, looking around the crowd to see if he could find his brother before Raphael could get to Emery.

Chapter 10

J ake led Emery through the sea of silk ties and beaded dresses. Her mind replayed the image of Luca's troubled face. He looked genuine, but he did not explain why he was concerned. *Could it have been an act?* Emery carried her doubts with her through the double French doors and outside into the cool evening.

"I thought you might like some fresh air," Jake said.

They stood at the precipice of an elevated patio overlooking a moonlit garden with a cobblestone path that zigzagged through the courtyard, spilling out into the streets of Medellín. The sounds of the city echoed off the hotel walls, and yet the courtyard felt peaceful. Quiet. Safe. Emery looked up at Jake and smiled gratefully.

"It's beautiful, thanks. I needed to get out of there."

She leaned her hip against the waist-high stone wall and looked up at the stars. Her mind wandered back to Luca and how he felt when he pressed his hand against her back as they danced. She shuddered all the way down her spine.

"You cold?" Jake asked.

"No, I'm fine."

"You got a thing for Romeo back there?"

"Who, Luca? No! Of course not." Emery brushed off his

question.

"That guy reeks of ulterior motives. You should stay away from him from now on."

Emery was perturbed at Jake's controlling instructions, but she stifled her irritation. Her practical side took over. The more time she spent away from Luca, and away from the champagne, the more she could think clearly.

It's not like she was looking for love in Colombia in the first place. Luca was all wrong for her. The spark she had felt with him must have been the champagne.

"Do you want to go for a walk?" Jake offered.

"I think that's exactly what I need."

Jake beamed. "Great!" he exclaimed. "But first, do you need a drink?"

"I think I'll pass on this round."

"Well, I need one. I'll be *right* back," Jake said as he headed through the doors.

A slight breeze sent goosebumps up her arms. Emery resituated herself against the stone wall with her arms crossed. She watched the flowers in the courtyard dance in the moonlight, and she regained her sense of calm.

Her mind wandered back to Luca, but she closed her eyes to shut him out.

Suddenly a rough hand clamped down on her shoulder, causing Emery to jerk her head. A strange man in a dirty cowboy hat stood beside her, looking out at the courtyard.

"May I have a word with you in private?" the stranger said.

Emery scrambled to find a response and stumbled over her tongue. The man didn't wait for her to answer and took her by the arm, away from the patio and onto the cobblestone path of the courtyard.

Emery tried to resist the man's grasp, and he only returned her attempts with a tighter grip. He was breathing heavily as he continued to steer Emery toward the shadows. His breath smelled of cigars and stale liquor. She didn't know if she should scream or kick, but before she could react, she was pushed against a stone wall at the edge of the courtyard. Low thumping sounds of a harmonic bass reverberated through the building's structure. Even if she wanted to scream, no one would hear her.

"I wasn't expecting a lady," the man said as he rubbed the back of his neck with one hand. "I may need to change my approach."

Emery's lip shook. She wanted to yell for help, but nothing would come out.

"It has come to my attention there has been a mistake."

Emery tried to regain her composure, but still, nothing would come out of her paralyzed mouth.

"You see, it makes no sense that your company would put on such a fancy party when times are hard. Eating caviar tonight and stealing from farmers tomorrow seems a little questionable, no?" He shoved a finger onto Emery's chest in the center of her breastbone, pinning her against the wall. His finger lingered, sliding down the deep neckline of her dress.

Emery trembled under his touch. His hot breath tickled her nose as he inched closer to her face. He removed his calloused finger and fiddled with her chandelier earring.

"Listen, I—" Emery started to plead.

"No," the man interrupted. "You listen to me!" He pressed his weight onto Emery, pinning her with his groin. His hands clasped around her neck. "You're going to listen to me," he repeated with conviction.

Smack!

Emery blinked and found the stranger crumpled on the ground. Disoriented, she looked up. Luca was standing over the man's body, gasping for breath and holding his right fist.

"Ow!" Luca hissed.

"Luca?" Emery gasped.

"There are more of them. We need to go," Luca demanded. "Now."

He held out his hand while he nervously surveyed the courtyard. Emery stared at it in fear. *Could she trust him? Where was Jake?*

Shouting voices sprang from the patio deck and echoed off the courtyard walls.

"One of them has a gun," Luca whispered. "We have to go, now!"

She hesitantly reached out her hand and placed it in his palm.

"Vamanos." He guided Emery through the shadows and into the streets of the city.

Chapter 11

Luisa opened the back door to her house. It was late. The lights were off. Turning on the kitchen light, she set her purse down on the kitchen counter and opened the refrigerator. Too exhausted and stressed to eat, she closed the door.

It had been a long double shift at the restaurant, and she had spent most of the day worrying about what Fernando's father was going to do to him when he got back from Medellín. Raphael had a temper like no other man she knew, and there was no conceivable way that he would accept her and Fernando's relationship after the accident.

She walked down the hallway toward her bedroom to find her mother finishing up in the bathroom.

"Luisa. How was your day?" her mother asked, standing in her nightgown.

"Exhausting. How was yours?" Luisa yawned.

"No bueno. Your father left behind a mess of things at the car shop. I don't know who is more miserable. Him, sitting in jail all day. Or me, cleaning up his finances."

"Lo siento, Mama."

"Ah well. You go on and get to bed, dear. I'll see you in the morning." She gave Luisa a kiss on the forehead and trudged to her bedroom.

Luisa opened her door. The moonlight flowed through her window, illuminating her bed and dresser. A dark figure emerged and grabbed her arm.

Luisa's adrenaline spiked, and she was about to scream when another hand covered her mouth.

"Shh. Luisa, it's me," Fernando whispered in her ear.

Luisa's breath normalized and Fernando let down his hand. *Smack!* Luisa's hand landed on his right cheek.

"You scared me to death, Fernando!"

Fernando tended to his wounded cheek before he could say anything in return. Luisa was filled with instant regret.

"Perdón, perdón, perdón." She kissed his cheek over and over. "Lo siento," she whispered, softly caressing his cheek.

The moonlit shadows on Fernando's face illuminated a forgiving smile.

"Why are you here?"

"I couldn't wait to see you again. I need you, Luisa."

His whisper sent shivers down her spine. Excitement and nervousness built low in her belly.

"Come back with me. Both my father and uncle are gone for the night."

"Fernando … I …"

"This might be our only chance to be alone. Please."

Luisa looked into his round, desperate eyes. He was so beautiful, even in the dark. She wanted him too, but they had never slept together before. Fernando would be her first.

She held his gaze as she shyly nodded her head.

Fernando grabbed her hand and led her through the pitch-black house, bumping into furniture all the way out. He had brought his dirt bike and parked it down the street.

"You want me to get on *that*?" she asked.

Fernando gave her a heart-melting smile and nodded vigorously as he handed her a helmet.

"You better know what you're doing," she said, strapping on the helmet.

Fernando got on the bike and scooched forward, giving her some room.

"Well, if I'm going to die tonight, at least I'll have a handsome man in my arms while I do it."

Fernando looked over his shoulder and gave her a kiss on the cheek.

"Hang on," he said, turning on the bike and kicking up the kickstand. Luisa winced at the rumbling sound, hoping it didn't wake her mother.

They sped down the streets and onto the country path. The stars overhead kept watch over them as they made their way to the plantation.

Fernando fumbled through his keys to find the right one for his uncle's door.

"Will your uncle mind that we are in his house?" Luisa asked.

"He wouldn't be as mad as my father. I'll just put it that way."

He opened the door to his uncle's house, and the living room was dark. He walked over to a side table and turned on the lamp.

It was a bachelor's house with the barest of necessities. One brown-colored couch and a small coffee table stood alone in a bare-walled room. The only other nearby furniture was a tattered blue reclining chair next to a small side table with an unfinished glass of liquor.

The warm glow from the lamp gave away Fernando's heated look of desire. He was biting his lip and walked to her. He reached over and unbuttoned the front of her dress, letting the sleeves fall from the tops of her shoulders.

Luisa breathed heavily as she pulled his T-shirt over his head. His smooth, caramel skin glowed in the lamplight, and she couldn't resist touching his chest. His body was perfect.

The desire in Fernando's eyes grew stronger as her dress fell to the floor.

"Te quiero," Fernando whispered.

Their lips joined in a fury of passion. Luisa's hands clung to Fernando's hair as they stumbled their way onto the couch.

He laid her down gently, placing a couch pillow under her head. Then he leaned in and softly kissed her neck. Her collarbone. Her rib cage. Her belly button. The soft spot just above her underwear. She squirmed, the tickling sensation making her body shiver under his touch. She cupped his chin, bringing him back to her lips. She kissed him fervidly, caressing his tongue, nibbling on his lower lip. As she tilted her hips up to meet his, Fernando looked deep into Luisa's eyes.

"You are the most beautiful thing in this world."

Chapter 12

Jake smiled, thinking of the way Emery had looked in her dress tonight. He had never seen her so sexy. Her deep plunging neckline had been taunting him all evening. He hoped to see more of her silky skin later tonight, if she would let him.

As Jake approached the outside balcony, his pace slowed to a halt in front of the wall where he had last seen Emery. He glanced around, but she was nowhere to be found.

Echoes of rowdy men arguing from across the courtyard caught his attention. As he slowly tipped one of the champagne flutes to his lips, he listened to their conversation in Spanish.

"What the hell happened, eh?"

"My brother. That bastard! He came out of nowhere!"

The group of men walked up to the balcony. The color of sun-faded jeans and dirty cowboy boots came into view.

Jake gulped.

When he looked up, the group of men was staring at him with targeted interest. One of the men was petting his mustache while looking Jake up and down.

A man wearing an off-white cowboy hat took a step forward, his eyes as sharp as daggers. His curly hair was sloppily tucked behind his ears, and an inflamed welt sat below his right eye.

It looked fresh.

"Lookie here, boys," the man taunted. "It's Emerson's little lap dog."

Jake curled his lip with confusion. "Qué?"

The man strutted toward him, popping his knuckles one at a time.

"Hey, hey, hey, fellas. What seems to be the trouble?" Jake asked as he raised his hands in surrender.

"We need a word with Emerson," said one of the men.

"She has some explaining to do," slurred another.

Jake tugged at the collar of his undershirt. "Well now, boys, maybe I can help you. I work for Emerson, and I'm sure we can talk this out."

Jake carefully took a small step backward. He studied the men staring back at him. They looked very angry, and drunk.

"What are you," The man wearing the cowboy hat strutted closer toward Jake. "Her secretary or something?"

The group of men laughed among themselves.

Jake scoffed. "Cute," he mocked. "I'm the senior director of supply," he said, making sure he carefully annunciated each syllable.

The man looked back to his group with amusement. "Is that right?" he said to his gang before returning to Jake. "This is good." He nodded. "This is very good." A sinister look appeared across the man's face, obliterating every last bit of confidence Jake had.

"You're coming with us," the man growled, slapping a firm grip on Jake's shoulder.

Jake was swept up in the flurry of men as two of them put their arms around his shoulders and walked through the courtyard and across the street.

The bar was dimly lit and smelled of booze and cigarette smoke. A pinball machine was placed in the far back corner with flashing colored lights reflecting off tables and chairs.

Jake looked back at the door and found himself eye to eye with the man petting his mustache, shaking his head. There was no way he could escape now.

Jake gave him a sheepish smile and shrugged before turning around to his doom.

The leader of the drunken henchmen twirled his finger to signal the bartender for a round of drinks as the other men grabbed chairs, pulling them toward an oversized round table in the back corner of the bar.

"Hey!" the leader said, snapping his fingers at Jake. "Pay the man," he ordered as he grabbed a stack of shot glasses and two large brown bottles.

Jake looked at the bartender, pleading with his eyes for help, but the bartender ignored Jake's silent prayer and lifted his palm to accept Jake's money.

Jake fumbled around in his pockets for his wallet. "How much?" he asked disconcertedly.

"Five hundred pesos," the man muttered.

Jake flipped through the colored paper money in his wallet and handed the bartender the cash.

"Ay, gringo!"

The men motioned for him to take the empty seat in their circle. He reluctantly sat next to the man in the cowboy hat. Alcohol was poured into each shot glass and passed around the table.

"Senior director of supply, eh?" The man smirked. "Can I ask you something?" He took off his cowboy hat and placed it on the corner of a chair. "Why has your company started a new round of negotiations?"

Jake thought about what to say for a few stolen moments. He reached out for an empty glass and waited for the man to fill his drink.

"Well, Mr. ..." Jake was stalling.

"Raphael," he answered. "Raphael Mendoza."

"I take it you all are farmers then?" Jake asked, looking around the table.

The men nodded, except for Raphael.

"Sí! Now give me an answer, goddammit!" Raphael barked.

Jake took a casual sip of his drink, letting the cheap liquor burn down his chest and into the pit of his belly. He fought the urge to cough it up.

"Mr. Mendoza," he said patiently. "The reason we have to go through another round of negotiations is because our company is not making enough money this year."

Jake took another sip, growing confident in his ability to swallow without wincing.

"If we can't hit our revenue and margin targets, the shareholders get pissed, and our stock price drops. You know how it is." Jake leaned back in his chair. "It's a terrible mess back at home base."

The group of men erupted with roaring laughter.

"I don't think I'm making myself clear. If we don't hit our plan, then we have to shift the type of supply we take in," Jake insisted. "This directly impacts you guys as well. Especially if we have to buy from Brazil or somewhere else."

Raphael rubbed his nose with his index finger. "So you mean to tell me that the only two options you have are to cut costs or stop doing business with us?"

Jake nodded.

"So the coffee farmers here are going to lose, no matter what?" Raphael raised his voice and slammed his empty glass on the table.

As if signaled, the bartender came around with a new bottle and placed it at the center.

Raphael looked at the bartender and nodded. "Keep it coming," he said, winking at Jake. "Senior director of supply has the tab. Right, amigo?"

Jake stiffened.

Raphael raised his glass. "Here's to a good run in the coffee business."

The men raised their glasses in the air with him. "May it rest in peace." All at once they took a drink and looked down at their empty shot glasses in despair.

Jake had left his drink on the table, but Raphael threatened him with a snarled lip. Jake sheepishly took the shot glass and whispered "bottoms up" under his breath. He tilted his head back and let the burning sensation coat his throat.

"I didn't catch your name, amigo," Raphael said.

"It's Jake."

"Yake?" Raphael snorted.

Jake chuckled over his glass. "Sure."

"If your company has no other option but to cut costs or cut Colombia out," a burly man interjected, "how could you afford a fancy party like that back there?"

"That party was put on by the Coffee Farmers Association. Coffee Benz didn't pay … for all of it."

The men shook their heads in disgust.

"This is bullshit!" roared Raphael. The shadow returned to his eyes. "Your people don't realize what the last round of cuts did to us! Or what it did to the shit coffee you are drinking now."

Raphael counted the reasons on each finger. "We're forced to buy the cheapest pesticides. The cheapest supplies. The cheapest pickers. And then after all that garbage, we combine our coffee beans with bags of fertilizer to cut costs on transportation." Raphael pounded on the table. "Do you hear me, gringo? Your coffee beans ride in a truck full of shit before they get to you!"

Jake sat quietly while the next round of drinks was being poured. Although the tension still existed among them, something changed. Raphael's tone went from raging mad to subdued anger with a dash of sadness. In fact, it was starting to seem like these men were just looking for someone to talk to. Someone from corporate who would actually listen.

Jake raised his glass. "To the fine gentlemen here who have found the courage to tell me what was actually going on." He turned his attention to Raphael and looked him straight in the eye. "I respect your fair questions, and I appreciate you confiding in me so I can take your feedback to headquarters. I will do everything I can to help you guys out." Jake tilted his head back with the glass against his lips and slammed his drink. He looked around at the gruff faces as they stared in silence.

Raphael smiled and patted him on the shoulder, raising his glass. "To our new friend!"

"Salud!" the men cheered.

***

Jake lost track of time. The stream of booze never stopped. The group of men became so loud that Jake barely noticed when a crowd of people walked through the tavern door, some wearing colorful costumes and flower-adorned hats. As the noise level elevated, the men peered over to the multicolored bunch, eyeing a particularly beautiful Colombian woman with a costume accentuating her voluptuous figure.

"Ay, mami!" said one of the men as he playfully wiped the brow of his forehead.

Raphael squinted at the woman. Their eyes locked. She sauntered toward them in her high heels. Raphael curled his lips into a Cheshire cat grin.

"Esmeralda," he purred as he opened his arms for a hug.

Smack! The young woman slapped her hand along the side of Raphael's cheek and in the same motion admired her freshly painted fingernails. Jake studied her with increasing interest. The lady pouted her lips as if she felt guilty at first, but then quickly got over it and smiled.

Raphael held his eye contact with the woman and lightly touched the pink patch that appeared on his face. Raphael's intensity seemed to soften as he smiled back.

"That was for your brother," the woman stated defiantly. "He didn't call me back." Esmeralda looked around the table and stuck out her bottom lip. "I see he's not here with you?"

"No," Raphael responded. "He's taking care of business at the moment."

"Who's the white boy?" Esmeralda asked as she sashayed toward Jake. Jake's spine went stiff. She leaned over him, slowly allowing him to drink in her flowery perfume, her cleavage only inches from his face. She bit the bottom corner of her lip and traced her long fingernail from Jake's temple to the bottom of his chin. "He's pretty handsome," she said. "For a white boy."

"His name is Yake," Raphael said, sitting back down in his chair and beckoning for one of his friends to refill his glass.

"Hola," the woman cooed.

"Hi." Jake gulped.

Esmeralda threw her head back, laughing.

"Relax, white boy, you are not my type," she said, laughing to herself. She reached over the bar table and grabbed a wide square bottle.

"Now, who wants some guaro?" she shouted.

Cheers roared from around the table.

Chapter 13

Emery was asleep in the passenger seat. She looked so peaceful, Luca hated to wake her. He cringed as he turned onto a gravel road, the rocking of the truck stirring Emery out of her dream.

"Where are we?" Emery asked.

"My cousin's farm," Luca said. He was unsure of how Nicholas would feel about being awakened in the middle of the night.

Luca parked his car in front of the house. "Wait here," Luca said, stepping out of the truck. He walked up to the front door and gave a few soft taps. Finally, a light went on and the door creaked open.

"Que pasa?" Nicholas appeared from behind the door.

"Nicholas. I am sorry to wake you. I need a place to stay tonight. Actually, we need a place to stay tonight," Luca said as he pointed toward the truck. Emery looked like a deer in headlights through the windshield.

Nicholas gave him a criticizing glare.

"It's not like that. It's a long story. I'll tell you tomorrow. Do you mind if we stay in your loft above the stables?"

"Of course. Whatever you need, cousin."

"Gracias. Mucho."

The loft apartment was a modest one, even by Luca's standards. It rested above the horses' stables, and it smelled as such. The wood flooring had survived years of neglect, and the once-painted-white coating had yellowed with age.

Emery walked to the middle of the dusty living area and looked around the room. She was shimmering like a golden goddess in the moonlight. The juxtaposition of her stark elegance against the rickety loft made Luca embarrassed for having taken her there.

"Perhaps we should find somewhere else to stay?" he asked, holding his breath for her reaction.

"This will be fine." Emery nodded as she tiredly tucked a strand of hair behind her ear. "Assuming I am safe here?"

"Sí. You are safe. You can sleep on the bed. I will take the couch," Luca said as his gaze shifted to the tattered and stained loveseat in front of a small television set with long metal antennas.

Emery nodded and approached what looked like an over-sized closet that held a full-size bed and a small dresser. She plopped herself at the edge of the bed. The springs in the mattress fought back against her weight, and the bed squeaked as she bounced up and down.

"There should be some clothes in the dresser for you to sleep in," Luca called out to her. She was staring off into the distance, appeared to be lost in her thoughts.

Instinctively he walked to her. Sounds of rotting hardwood squeaked under his steps. Emery looked up and gave him a wary smile.

Luca sat on the bed, and the springs of the mattress sent them in the air, bouncing up and down.

Emery giggled. "Thank you for taking me here."

Luca sighed and looked around the room. The sheer curtains draped around the little window above the bed, laced with holes and stains. The bedding was covered in dust, and it smelled of horse manure.

"Well, it isn't Colombia's finest establishment," he joked, "but it will do."

"It's great," she reassured him. Her soft hand cupped the tops of his knuckles.

A flash of Raphael clutching Emery's neck in the shadows of the night crept into Luca's mind, and his muscles tightened. Anger festered deep in his stomach at the thought of anyone hurting her. What Raphael did was unforgivable.

Emery's facial expression mirrored the same thoughts going through Luca's head.

"Are you okay?" Luca asked tenderly.

Tears built up in Emery's eyes until they dropped freely, streaking her rosy cheeks as they streamed down onto her lap. The skin around her neck and chest became blotchy red, and she covered her face with her hands.

Wrapping his arms around her, he cradled her head onto his chest. He cupped the back of her neck and lightly tightened his arms securely around her. Her body relaxed in his embrace, submitting to his protective hold.

"Lo siento," Luca whispered delicately.

He could feel her warmth through his shirt. He continued to hold her through her quiet sobs until the shaking of her body settled into soft sniffles.

Emery pulled herself up, and Luca reluctantly let her go. The warmth she left on his chest slowly evaporated, leaving Luca yearning for more.

He cupped his hand around her ear, letting his thumb lightly brush the side of her cheek. Emery responded and leaned into his hand. Her lips were so close, the heat of her breath tickled his chin. Her kiss was imminent, but he froze.

Something inside screamed for him to stop. He broke away from her gaze and abruptly stood.

"You should get some sleep," he heard himself say.

What the hell was he doing? When he looked back at Emery, she was looking the other way, wiping off her tears. "Good night," Luca said, walking out the door.

"Luca—"

His heart started to race. He turned toward her, steadying his breath. "Sí?"

She studied him for a moment and gave a weak smile.

"Good night," she said.

Luca tossed and turned on the dusty loveseat throughout the night. The memory and heat of Emery's touch plagued his heart. The moonlight penetrated his eyelids even though they were clenched shut. Grabbing a dusty pillow, he placed it over his face. The impact of the pillow forced a light cloud of dust into his lungs. It smelled like mothballs and mud. He coughed and threw the pillow on the ground, repositioning himself across the armrest of the loveseat. His neck wrapped over one of the scroll arms, and his knees fought against the side of the other.

The loveseat jabbed him at every angle regardless of how he lay, and he couldn't stop thinking of the way Emery looked at him just moments before his good sense ruined it all. Her pouty lips, her inviting eyes. She was welcoming him to take her.

Creeeaaaaak. A sound of wood broke the midnight silence, and he sharply raised his head over the back of the couch. He stared at the closed door of the small bedroom and silently prayed for Emery to open it.

A shadow moved under the door sill, and Luca's heart jumped. He waited and listened for her to come out, but the silence was only broken by the light squeaky sounds of the mattress springs echoing from behind the bedroom door.

"I'm such an idiot," Luca whispered to himself, and he huffed to one side, wishing for sleep to take him away.

Luca didn't realize he fell asleep until the neighing sound of a horse knocked him out of his drooling slumber. He nervously wiped the corners of his mouth and looked around the room, not sure if he had an audience.

Daylight poured lazily through the windowpanes in beams of light, showing every dust particle dancing in the air. He carefully stood up from the couch and felt every muscle ache. Luca knocked softly on the bedroom door at the edge of the living area. He waited, but there was no answer. He knocked a little harder. Nothing. Luca's heart started to pound.

"Emery? You in there?" He reached for the doorknob and opened the door slowly. He poked his head from the crack and quickly scanned the small bedroom. She was gone.

Shit.

He grabbed the keys resting on the small end table near the front door, and he combed his hand through his hair. Ripping the apartment door open, he rushed down the squeaky wooden steps.

Luca bit the top of his knuckle and tried to think. *Where the hell could she have gone? Could something have happened to her? Where was he going to look?*

Soft feminine laughter echoed from the stables.

"You see," said a man's voice. "You're quite the natural."

Luca walked through the aisle of the stables and around the corner to where wooden posts and chicken wire had been placed in a large circular perimeter. Old rotting wood was stacked and propped against each other like a fence. His cousin was leaning against the stable beam. Nicholas's attention was focused inside. He shifted his sight to Luca and nodded stoically and redirected his attention.

Luca followed his cousin's gaze. His blood pressure equalized the instant he saw her. Emery sat on the loose dirt with a colt resting in her lap. The young horse was kneeling into her while she softly petted his neck.

"You had me worried, I—" Luca stopped midsentence. Emery was wearing what looked like a gigantic bedsheet of a T-shirt, billowing into equally large overalls. The edges of Luca's heart melted at the sight. The sun accentuated a golden aura around her, the strands of her hair blowing wildly in the morning breeze.

Luca smiled.

"I see you've met my cousin, Nicholas," Luca said.

"I did. He was just telling me about Azul here. He's such a friendly little guy," she said as she kissed the colt's snout. "The horse is sweet too."

Emery winked. Her face was beaming. She couldn't have looked more adorable if she had tried.

"How about I take you to town so we can get some proper clothes," Luca suggested.

He watched Emery ponder the idea.

"We can come back and pet the horses after," he reassured her.

Emery gave the horse a brief kiss on the forehead and jumped to her feet, dusting the clouds of dirt off of her clothes. Luca laughed.

"Are you sure you don't like my outfit?" she teased.

"There's something I want to show you," he said as he extended his hand and offered it to her.

"I guess we have time," she said with a smile.

***

It was a beautiful morning. The birds were chirping, and the sun shone brightly on the green hilltops in the distance. Emery rolled her window down and let the crisp morning air fill her lungs, her hair dancing wildly around her face. The lush and green scenery took her breath away with every passing mile.

They drove alongside a goat farm. Goats with perturbed looks on their faces and tufts of grass hanging out of their mouths came into view. Emery giggled at their funny expressions.

"Never seen goats before?" Luca asked.

"I have, but these look downright grumpy!" She chuckled. "I don't know what they have to be grumpy about. This is the most beautiful place I have ever seen."

"It's not so bad here." Luca smiled as he focused his attention back on the road.

Emery studied the side of Luca's face while he continued to drive them down the dirt road. He carried a proud smile that touched Emery's heart.

She thought about the concrete jungle back in Chicago. The tall skyscrapers towered in the sky. The city was busy and overpopulated with people walking and driving along stained concrete roads.

"Have you ever been to Chicago?" Emery asked.

"I can't say I have."

"Have you been to the States at all?"

"Actually, no. I haven't traveled outside of Colombia before." Emery tilted her head in surprise.

"Really? You've never left once?" she pressed.

Luca shook his head. "Do you travel a lot?"

"I have traveled, yes. There's not much time for it nowadays, but I love exploring other countries. Rome had been my favorite place I've visited."

"Had been?" Luca asked.

"Until I came here."

Luca flashed his dimples, causing Emery to feel warm and fuzzy inside. She looked out at the small wooden shacks covered in cardboard and old rugs. Laundry hung off lines between makeshift posts. Children ran through the huts and played with sticks as if they were swords.

"Who are these people?" Emery asked.

"This is where the coffee pickers live."

Emery's heart felt heavy with guilt. "They wouldn't be picking for Coffee Benz, right?"

"Well, I don't know for sure. But they most likely work for my cousin, and his farm sells to Coffee Benz. So they probably are."

"How can this be? I thought we paid well enough above the market average," Emery said, sick to her stomach. "This doesn't add up."

"What kind of living conditions do you think the market average provides?"

"I guess I don't really know." Emery shook her head.

"Well, now you know what 'above the market average' looks like," Luca said as he turned down a street toward San Pedro's city center.

"We're here, but it looks like the shop is closed. Want to get some coffee while we wait?" Luca asked.

"I'd like that," Emery said, still pensive from her recent discovery.

Emery and Luca pulled up in front of a small wood-framed building. The cafe had an intricate wrought-iron filigree surrounding the glass pane windows. A weathered sign swayed in the breeze that read Las Montañas Cafe hanging above a green front door.

Emery walked up to the shop and reached for the door handle, but Luca quickly propped the door open and welcomed her to the wafting aroma of fresh coffee beans and baked goods. The cafe was filled with a dozen small round tables with red and white plastic tablecloths. The walls were decorated with old black and white photos of Colombian farmers in the coffee fields standing in front of their homes.

"Buenos días," said the man behind the counter. "What can I get you?"

"Two coffees, por favor," Luca said, placing a few pesos on the counter.

Luca guided Emery to the back corner. As they sat down, the server placed two small cups of coffee on the table.

"Gracias," Emery said.

Luca was holding back a chuckle, and he motioned for her to pick up her coffee.

"What's so funny?"

Luca smiled, showing Emery his dimples.

"Oh, nothing," Luca teased. "Your accent is cute."

Emery raised her eyebrows. "Cute?"

"Sí. It sounds like you're saying 'grassy ass.'"

"Gra-ci-as," she said again.

"You sound like a sick cat."

Emery acted aghast.

"A cute sick cat," he corrected.

They both laughed and took their first sips of coffee.

Emery closed her eyes and hummed with delight. The hot coffee was earthy and sweet. She savored it, enjoying the smooth finish. "I needed you," she said to her cup. "I don't think I could have lasted another minute without you."

Luca cocked an eyebrow. "Did you just talk to your coffee?"

"So what if I did?" Emery teased.

"Then this is the first time I've ever been jealous of a cup of coffee."

Emery blushed.

"It's good coffee. It's amazing how much richer it tastes here."

"Sí, this is not bad. But there is a slight metallic aftertaste. Can you tell?" Luca asked as he took another sip.

Emery pulled another drink from the porcelain cup. She let the coffee coat her palate and focused on the bitterness that lingered when she swallowed.

"You're right," she said. "Why is that?"

"This coffee was either kept in a metal container at some point, or it's the residue from the chemicals used on the coffee."

"I see."

"A couple of years ago, there was a round of price cuts," Luca began.

Emery nodded. "I remember. I was working in a different department then, but everyone knew."

"Well, all the farmers had to cut their production costs to stay above water. That meant that they had to switch their brands of pesticides and cleaning agents. Everyone buys the low-grade stuff now. A lot of farmers cut down the time to wash the beans too, which means we're drinking remnants of chemicals that aren't getting washed off properly."

"Are you serious? I didn't think it would impact the taste *that* much. But now that you mention it, that explains a lot about the quality issues we've been having recently."

Luca nodded.

Emery continued to work through the issue in her mind. They sat in comfortable silence for a little while, drinking their coffee and occasionally sharing a friendly smile.

"Hey, how about we go into the shop now and get you something other than those dusty overalls to wear?" Luca asked, taking in his last drops of coffee.

"I've grown rather fond of the roominess," Emery joked.

They waved goodbye to the cafe owner and walked over to the clothing shop just as an older lady was unlocking it from the other side. When they walked in, the bell on the door chimed a pleasant chirping sound.

Emery glanced around the room of circular racks full of vibrantly colored clothes. There were costume dresses, pajama sets, and workwear all on the same rack. As she walked around the shop, she couldn't help but notice that Luca held his gaze on her.

Emery grabbed a few dresses and tucked each item under her arm.

"Would you like to try these things on?" the older lady asked kindly. "Vamos. Follow me, and I'll show you where to change."

Emery followed the old lady behind a row of racks in a darkened corner of the room with a tiny mirror balanced along the wall. Luca stalked slowly behind.

"Here you go. Go ahead and try them on," said the store manager.

Emery glanced at the changing area and raised her eyebrows. The only hope she had of privacy was a low-hanging, thinly draped curtain.

"I'll stand guard," Luca said with a nod and turned his back to Emery.

Emery pulled on a bright blue dress. It was different than her normal white-and-beige attire. An A-line skirt stopped just above her knees and swayed beautifully as she moved from side to side. She was admiring herself in the mirror when Luca appeared in the corner of her eye, peeking through the gaping hole through the flimsy curtain.

"Hey!" Emery called out, pushing the curtain to the side and pointing a finger directly at Luca. "You were peeking!" Emery scolded.

Luca threw his hands up in surrender, but his eyes rested on her dress.

"That dress looks …" Luca trailed off breathlessly.

"Shoo!" Emery pulled the curtain back. Her face was warm, and she smiled to herself, thinking of Luca's reaction. She looked down at the small mirror in the corner and twirled to the side one last time.

This is the one. She grinned.

"Why don't you go wait outside? I won't be much longer," Emery said through the curtain.

"Sí, señorita."

Emery walked out to find Luca leaning against the wall of the brick building next door.

"You look beautiful."

"Gra-ci-as," Emery said with a wide grin. "What now?"

"Let's head back. I want to introduce you to Nicholas's wife, Maria. You're going to love her. She'll probably try to plump you up. She loves to cook."

"Works for me. Perhaps I'll be able to fit in those overalls after all."

Chapter 14

Rows of coffee trees nestled on the west side of the farmhouse. A field of flowers rested on the east side. Pinks, reds and yellows popped through the field of green. Several field workers wearing large white-brimmed hats fanned out across the fields, tending to their floral children.

Luca and Emery walked up to the house. A man talked loudly into the telephone.

Luca knocked on the front door, which was covered in layers of white paint chipping off in big chunks. When the door opened, a familiar face greeted them. It was Luca's cousin, Nicholas. His big rosy cheeks and teddy-bear body with open arms welcomed them in.

"Sí, I understand," Nicholas said into the wireless phone pressed against his ear. "Did you check your neighbors'?"

Emery and Luca stepped into the foyer of the farmhouse and waited for Nicholas to finish his conversation.

"Claro. I'll let you know if I see him. Hasta luego." Nicholas hung up the phone and gave Luca a suspicious look. "You want to tell me what's going on?"

"Who was that?" Luca asked.

"It was Raphael. He's looking for you and someone named

Emerson."

Luca's eyes grew wide.

"Who's Raphael?" Emery asked. "And how does he know I'm with you?"

Nicholas looked at Luca, who was rubbing his neck.

"Emery. Raphael is the man I knocked out last night. The man who—"

"The man who attacked me? You know him?"

Luca nodded. "Emery—"

"The coffee farmers around here know each other," Nicholas chimed in. "Especially the ones who work with Coffee Benz. We all know about the negotiations, and we talk. Some of us know how to handle it better than others. Raphael is definitely someone who can't handle it. And he's got a crew of men looking for you both. They don't know you're here. So you're safe now."

Emery's stomach plummeted. "I don't know what to say."

"Just say you'll stay. One more night," Luca pleaded. "You heard Nicholas. It's not safe to go back to the city just yet."

Emery bit her lip while she thought it over.

"I don't want to impose," Emery started.

"No imposition at all. Let us show you around the coffee farm. You may learn a few things you can take back to headquarters," Nicholas said, giving her a wink.

Emery nodded politely. "Okay. I'll do it. If you're sure I won't be inconveniencing you?"

Nicholas laughed. "Inconveniencing me? Not at all. My wife will be thrilled to have you here for dinner tonight."

Dinner tonight? Oh, crap. She was supposed to be having dinner with Jake back in the city.

"Do you mind if I make a call?"

"Claro," Nicholas said, leading her to an office in the back of the house.

***

Nicholas stormed back into the kitchen. "What the hell is going on?" he demanded. "You didn't tell her Raphael is your brother?"

Luca sighed. "I was about to."

"I'm trying to save your ass. If you haven't told her by now, it's too late." Nicholas ran his hands through his hair.

"The whole thing is a mess," Luca explained. "I came to the city to try to convince Emery to stop the negotiations. I thought I could get her away from the boardroom, but not like this." Luca scratched the stubble that was growing along his chin.

"Luca …" Nicholas said as he shook his head.

"Raphael showed up and had his hands around her neck. I panicked and knocked him out."

"Ay."

"You should have seen him. He had a whole clan with him too. I was worried it was going to become a mob, and Raphael was going to get blamed for it all." He trembled at the thought. "I had to get her out of there to save her, and save my brother from doing something stupid."

"I see," Nicholas said. "She's pretty, no?" Nicholas teased.

Luca tried his best to suppress a smile.

Nicholas laughed. "Your face says it all, primo."

Emery returned from the room with a look of disappointment.

"I had to leave a message with Jake. I was supposed to have a business dinner with him. I just wanted to make sure he knew I was okay."

Luca flinched at the sound of Jake's name. Jake's feelings toward Emery had become obvious at the gala last night. He had been trying to mark his territory all evening.

Just then a round woman walked in with two large paper sacks in her arms. Her cheeks looked like bright apples atop a round, happy face, and her black hair was tied up into a bun with a red scrunchie. When she looked up and saw Luca and Emery, her face beamed.

"Luca! It is so good to see you!" She hurried over to Luca and wrapped her arms around him and squeezed.

"Maria!" Luca choked through the squeezes. "It's good to see you too. Thank you so much for letting us stay last night." He shifted his gaze to Emery and smiled. "I'd like to introduce you to someone."

Maria clasped her hands over her mouth. "Dios mio! Aren't you just the prettiest thing?" Maria reached out to Emery's hand and led her into the kitchen. "I bet you are starving!"

"Oh, you don't have to—"

"Nonsense!" Maria exclaimed. "No one leaves my house hungry, isn't that right, Luca?"

Luca raised his eyebrows and smiled. "Sí. Maria, do you think it would be too much trouble if we stay one more night?"

"Of course not," Maria said as she unloaded fresh vegetables out of the paper sacks. "So what brought you all the way over here in the middle of the night?"

"It's a long story," Luca began.

"I was attacked at the gala last night," Emery chimed in. "Luca came to my rescue."

"About that—" Luca started.

"Praise Jesus!" Maria shouted. "I'm so glad Luca was there to save you!"

Nicholas glared from across the table.

"Actually, there is something I—" Luca began.

"What's for lunch, dear?" Nicholas interrupted, eyeing all the groceries on the counter.

"Sancocho," Maria hummed.

"What can I do?" Emery offered, holding a bushel of herbs in one hand and a large red onion in the other.

"Nothing, dear, thank you. Why don't you and Luca take a walk and be back in an hour for lunch?"

Emery seemed hesitant to leave, but Maria proceeded to shoo her and Luca out of the kitchen.

"I've got this," she gloated. "You two go have fun."

Chapter 15

"If you would like to leave a message, please wait for the tone. Beep."

"Hi Jake, it's me, Emery. I just wanted to let you know that I'm fine. I'm planning on coming back tomorrow. There was a man that attacked me at the gala. He has been calling around, so I don't feel safe enough to come back today. I'll try you again later."

Jake stirred in his hotel bed, wallowing in a hangover. He swore he heard the phone ring, but he couldn't tell if it was the phone or his head. The room spun, and he was pretty sure he was still drunk. Flashes of rum bottles, cigars, and dancing ladies in bright thongs came to mind.

Shit.

A pounding headache crept into his consciousness. He sat up in bed and groaned. Raphael and the crew of farmers had bonded at the tavern over shots of aguardiente, which apparently landed on his tab.

Crap. How was he going to explain that business expense to Emery? Emery!

He had found out that she had left with Luca, who was using her to save his farm. He was going to break her heart. Jake rubbed his temples, thinking of how he was going to break the news to her. First, he had to find her.

As he stepped out of bed, a rustling noise made him whip around. An ocean of black hair covered the pillow next to him.

What the—?

The mound of hair moved, and an arm swept it off her face.

Esmeralda?

How did she—?

Did we—?

Memories poured in. They were in an elevator, making out next to a quiet Japanese couple.

Oh God. Lipstick was everywhere.

Oh no. The mini bar.

Oh shit. Shoes flying. Clothes tearing. Esmeralda riding him like an old Western cowboy.

"Good morning, white boy," Esmeralda said in a gravelly voice.

"Good morning," Jake said uneasily, padding across the room toward his pants. He picked them up and dressed briskly.

Esmeralda's makeup from yesterday had migrated toward the right side of her face. Her eyeliner smudged around her right eye, and her hair pointed wildly in the direction of the ceiling light.

"Perhaps you might need the bathroom before I shower and head to the office?" Jake asked.

"I will in a minute. Why don't you sit by me and let me take care of you before you head to work?" Esmeralda said as she patted the bed next to her.

Jake was distracted by the lipstick running down her face. He wasn't sure if she was smiling or very, very sad.

"I would, Esmeralda, but I have to go. It's a bit of an emergency."

"I know all about your little emergency named Emery. You

wouldn't shut up about her last night. That is, until I shut you up." She winked.

"Can I get you a cab somewhere?" he said, slipping on his shoes, hoping to escort her out as quickly as possible.

"You're not getting rid of me that quickly, *lover*. We have unfinished business to tend to," she said, getting out of bed, about to pounce on her prey.

"Oh yeah? How so?" Jake said, inching his way toward the bathroom.

She continued to prowl and closed the gap between them as Jake stepped into the bathroom. She reached out to grab his jaw and caught a look of herself in the mirror.

"Aaaahhh!" she screeched. "Why didn't you tell me I was such a mess!" she said, grabbing a towel and hitting him with it.

"I didn't. Want. To hurt. Your feelings!" he said between towel swats.

"Awww. That's so sweet, white boy. You American boys are so nice," she said, giving him a kiss on the cheek. "Let me wash up. I've got my own emergency to tend to," she said, waving at the door before scrubbing her face.

Jake swallowed hard and stepped out of the bathroom.

Moments later, Esmeralda came out, clean-faced, and a dirty look in her eyes. She walked right past Jake and lay down on the bed.

"Come here, white boy. It's business time."

"No, really. I have to find Emery."

Esmeralda slowly spread her legs open.

Jake dropped his briefcase and floated to Esmeralda, letting his clothes drip from his body onto the floor.

Chapter 16

Fernando woke to the sounds of chirping in nearby trees outside the window. His arm wrapped possessively around the angelic creature lying beside him. He fluttered his eyes open to find Luisa sleeping peacefully in the glow of the morning light.

Dust in the bedroom shimmered in the air like a glittery fog. The cream-colored sheet barely covered Luisa's lower half, her perfect breasts only partially covered by her resting arm.

Fernando wanted to hold on to this moment forever. He would never be able to get enough of her. A familiar itch in his lungs beckoned him to cough, but he resisted the urge so as not to wake Luisa from her peaceful slumber. He watched her for a while, wondering if it was normal to be so in love at this age. He would do anything for her, even if it meant leaving home, away from his tyrant father.

Luisa's shoulder glistened against the sunbeam pouring through the window. He couldn't help himself and traced her golden skin with his finger. His soft touch sent instant goosebumps up her arms. She opened her eyes to find Fernando lovingly trailing down her back and around the curve of her slender hips.

"Good morning." She smiled.

"Good morning," Fernando returned, nibbling up her jawline toward her earlobe.

Luisa made a sweet humming sound that echoed in Fernando's heart. He recalled similar sounds she had made last night, and his chest filled with desire for her again. His growing need for her started to suffocate him. Pain deep in his lungs immediately took over. He let out the wretched cough he had been holding in, keeling over from the fiery pain shooting out of his chest and onto his pillow.

Blood splattered across the pillowcase. Luisa shot up in horror as Fernando lost control over himself, coughing and spitting blood into his hands.

"Fernando!" Luisa gasped. "What's happening?" She leapt out of the bed to put her hands on Fernando's back, trying to comfort him.

Fernando sat at the edge of the bed, helpless and shaking. He couldn't answer her. He couldn't breathe. He couldn't think of anything but the sharp knives splitting his insides.

The room darkened. He blinked to find Luisa's panicked face in front of him. She was calling to him. Crying for him, until his vision went black.

***

Raphael sat at the diner counter, covering his face with his hands. Forks dinged against porcelain plates, reverberating in his skull. The smell of eggs taunted his nauseous stomach.

When the waitress put a cup of coffee in front of him, the clash of the mug against the laminate countertop struck Raphael between the eyes. His head was going to split in two. He looked at the waitress through his fingers as if she had a death wish.

"You did a number on yourself last night," Carlos said, sitting beside him at the breakfast bar. Carlos's lips pressed against the hot coffee mug before taking in his first drink.

"I know, I know," Raphael said, grabbing his coffee.

They sat in silence. The large mirror behind the breakfast bar reflected the bustling restaurant behind them. People sat at booths, boisterously recounting the events from the prior night. Raphael watched begrudgingly at all the joyful faces through the mirror and willed them all to leave.

He looked defeatedly back into his coffee mug and stared at the black hole before taking another sip. Caffeine pumped through his veins, and memories of last night seeped their way into his consciousness.

"Did I see Esmeralda leave with Yake last night?" Raphael asked.

"Sí," Carlos said, straight-faced.

Raphael shook his head in disbelief.

He recalled setting things straight with Jake, who seemed to understand their situation, and even indicated that he would talk to his boss about pausing the negotiations. But Raphael needed to make sure Emerson would follow through.

"I'm going to make a few calls," Raphael said, walking to the waiting area with a pay phone and a phone book sitting on the side table next to it.

He searched his pockets for change before dialing his cousin's phone number.

"Hola?" Nicholas said on the other line.

"Primo. It's Raphael. Como estas?"

"Bueno. Tu?"

"I'm all right. I'm looking for my brother. Have you seen

him?"

There was a pause on the other line.

"Luca? No, I can't say I have. Is everything okay?"

"The guys and I are looking for him. He's run off with the woman in charge of the negotiations this week."

"He ran off with the woman, so what?" Nicholas chuckled on the other line.

"I don't know what side he's on anymore. I caught him schmoozing with the corporate gringos last night. He could be cutting a deal behind my back for all I know."

"Luca wouldn't—"

"Maybe not," Raphael interrupted, "but he would easily be swindled by that mujer. I don't trust him. I need to make sure that woman knows what she's getting herself into with cutting costs again. If I don't find her, one of the other farmers will."

"Sí. Yes, I understand," Nicholas said into the phone.

"The future of our farms depends on setting that Emerson woman straight. Keep your eyes open and let me know if you see or hear any signs of him."

"Si, I understand. Did you check your neighbors'?" Nicholas asked.

"No. I'm in Medellín now, but I will ask around."

"Claro. I'll let you know if I see him. Hasta luego."

"Hasta luego." Raphael let the phone rest on the receiver as he ran his fingers through his hair. He searched his pockets again. He needed to call his boys to make sure everything was in order at home. Fernando was supposed to be working in the office today.

He placed a few coins in the pay phone before dialing the office phone number. The phone rang without an answer, and Raphael's temper grew with each ring. The answering machine turned on, and Raphael slammed the phone.

He put in a couple more pesos and tried again. The voice mail picked up, and he dropped the phone from his ear, letting it hang. The sound of the answering machine recording echoed in the phone booth as Raphael stormed out.

"I need to head back to the plantation and check on things there."

Carlos nodded. "Sí. I'll let you know if I find Luca and the woman."

Raphael tipped his cowboy hat and walked out of the diner and down the street to his truck before peeling out of the city and into the countryside.

Chapter 17

Emery gazed at the landscape as Luca led her out of the farmhouse. The sun beamed high in the sky, only partially covered by big fluffy clouds. The air was warm and scented by the neighboring flowers.

Luca reached over and took Emery's hand to lead her into the rows of coffee trees. Warmth spread through her body at his touch. She watched him while he inspected the leaves and the coffee cherries.

"These look good enough to eat," Emery said, taking one between her fingers.

"They are actually quite sweet. You should try one."

"Really?"

Luca reached around her and pulled a ripe red cherry off the tree. He inspected it first before rubbing it on his shirt.

"Here," he said, handing it to her.

Emery placed the cherry in her mouth. The tart sensation made her mouth water.

"These are fine trees. Some of the best coffee in the world comes from this region. My cousin is very lucky to have inherited this farm."

Emery spat the coffee bean out into her hand and inspected it with a close eye. "It's amazing that this tiny little bean can be made into coffee."

"Sí. Only about seventy-nine more of those little beans and you can make one cup. All hand-picked for your pleasure," Luca said playfully.

"It's cute how proud you are of your work," Emery said.

"Well, many of us are proud of what we do. The coffee plants are like our children. We care for them. We want them to grow and prosper."

Emery smiled at the sparkle in Luca's eyes.

"Providing anything less than the best coffee is an insult to generations of coffee growers before us."

"Is it not the best now?"

"No," Luca said curtly.

"How do you mean?"

"Well, for one, we could be getting a better harvest if we were able to pay our pickers more. The wages we can afford don't allow us to retain good pickers. We end up with a bunch of unripened green cherries, which alters the taste."

"I had no idea." Emery frowned.

"And there are other things going on, corporate mandates and restrictions that Coffee Benz has imposed on us that add to our costs. We're all struggling to make a profit."

Emery scowled, feeling in over her head. How was she not aware this was going on?

"Conejita," Luca whispered. He embraced her in his arms, and she melted into him. She let the weight of her burden be shared with a man she hardly knew.

He clutched her to his chest before lifting her chin to his.

"You can change it. You can help us." His oceanic blue eyes were swimming with hope.

Emery wanted to believe him, but doubt ate at her soul.

"If you are the strong, independent woman that I'm getting to know, then I'm confident you can make things right."

With Luca's words, the seed of determination was planted in Emery's heart.

They continued to walk through the trees and down the sloping hills in silence as Emery tried to untangle the mess of their situation in her head. She held on to Luca's encouragement as if it were pulling her out of quicksand.

He believed in her. He needed her. All the farmers needed her.

Shades of pinks, yellows, and violets poked through the coffee trees.

"Is this Nicholas's land too?"

"Sí." Luca smiled.

Emery ran into the field of flowers and twirled around, letting the dazzling colors coat her vision until she plopped down into a grassy area. The ground was cool and damp, but Emery didn't care. She looked up at the puffy clouds in the sky and breathed in the fresh air.

Luca laughed as he trailed behind her and sat down. The clouds moved slowly overhead. Birds chirped in the distant trees, and Emery found a moment of peace.

"Have you always wanted to be a coffee farmer?" she asked.

"Sí. My father was a great farmer and a wonderful man. I always wanted to be like him."

A twinkling secret lingered on Luca's lips. Emery yearned to hear more. How was it possible to feel both relaxed and invigorated at the same time? He made her feel so comfortable. So alive.

"I loved planting the tiny trees as a kid. It took years for the ones I planted to produce cherries. The wait was agonizing, especially as a kid." Luca smiled as he played with a blade of grass. "But God, it was worth the wait."

She held on to his words for a moment, while he playfully tickled her nose with his blade of grass. "When the first cherry bloomed, it was the most amazing thing. I felt like," Luca paused to carefully choose his words. "I felt like I was part of something bigger than me, like I was doing God's work. I wouldn't consider myself a religious man, but when it comes to farming, I feel pretty close to God."

Emery batted her eyes, engrossed in every accented syllable that came out of his perfect mouth. "So what do you do when you're not growing coffee?" she asked.

"I love to spend time with my nephews. My brother has three boys. Fernando, who's seventeen now, and two twin boys, Juan and Mateo, who are fifteen years old. They are good kids. Their mother died in a car accident a few years ago, and my brother started drinking." Luca's thoughts trailed off with the wind while Emery studied his face. "So I take care of the boys. Fernando wants to take over the plantation one day, so I'm helping him get ready."

"I bet you are an amazing uncle."

"I don't know about that, but I love them as if they were my own. I feel responsible for them, given my brother's condition."

"Do you have a woman at home to help you with all that responsibility?" Emery asked, and immediately blushed at her own directness.

Luca laughed.

"No," he finally said. "I haven't been able to catch a conejita at home just yet." His dimples were on full display along with his flirty grin.

Emery playfully pushed him away.

"How about you? What do you do outside of being a big-time vice president for Coffee Benz?"

"I don't have much of a life outside of work either. I'm usually too busy to go out with friends, or to date."

"What about Jake?" Luca prodded.

Emery sighed. "I swear, there is nothing going on with Jake. He's just a friend from work who now reports to me. It would be terribly inappropriate."

Luca's jaw clicked. "Is that all that's stopping you? That it's inappropriate?"

Emery was caught off guard at his change in demeanor. "It's not just that. He's not…" She hesitated.

"Not what?"

You, she thought. She dared herself to say it.

"He's not …" Emery paused again. "He's not my type."

Luca's mood softened. "Well then, what *is* your type?" he asked.

She couldn't muster the strength to say it aloud. She stared into his eyes instead, wondering if he could read her thoughts. All the cells in her body shimmered. *Tell him! Tell him!*

The corner of Luca's mouth curled into a roguish grin, and he looked up toward the sun, shielding his eyes from the direct light.

"I think it's about time," he said, standing. "Let's head back to the house before Maria sends Nicholas looking for us." He held out his hand and swept her off her feet, throwing her over his shoulder.

"Luca! Put me down!" Emery laughed, pounding on his back.

He gave her a friendly pat on her backside, which was now pointed toward the sky.

"I hope Maria and Nicholas are hungry. I just caught us a little rabbit! Mi conejita!" He carried her up the hill, Emery squealing and laughing the entire way to the house.

Maria had just finished putting spoons and napkins on the table when she looked up to see them come in. The house smelled so delicious, Emery could have licked the table.

"Come in, come in! Get yourself some sancocho," she said, pouring soup from the pot into individual bowls.

"Maria, this looks delicious. How did you whip this up so fast?" Luca said, taking his bowl.

"I had prepped this yesterday. I just needed a few ingredients today to finish it up. Now eat! Eat!"

The rectangular wooden table was set with a plate of arepas and sliced avocados. Folded yellow paper napkins sat on top of a red, orange, and yellow floral tablecloth.

"Nicholas!" Maria cried out the window like a screeching cat. "Nicholas, it's time to eat!"

Luca and Emery grimaced at Maria's high-pitched call and giggled to each other. A moment later, Nicholas walked in with dirt all over his hands.

"What took you so long?" Maria snapped. "These poor kids have nearly starved to death waiting for you."

"Settle down. I was tending to the harvest," Nicholas said, brushing his nagging wife off to wash his hands in the sink.

Nicholas sat down at the head of the table and grabbed an arepa.

"Mmm," said Emery, taking a taste. "This is delicious, Maria. Thank you."

"You're so welcome, dear. I'm glad you like it," Maria said with a proud smile.

Nicholas told tales of his childhood with Luca. They used

to live on the same farm together until Nicholas took over Maria's father's farm several years ago. Nicholas was very expressive when he spoke, pounding the table for emphasis and raising his voice at the climactic parts of each story. Emery quickly decided that she liked Nicholas and Maria.

"And then one time, Luca thought it would be a great idea to climb that tree to save a cat," Nicholas said, laughing to himself. "You remember that, primo?"

"How can I forget." Luca rolled his eyes.

"This kid thought he was Spider-Man. It was pretty impressive to see him get all the way to the top branch where the cat was. But of course, Luca got stuck up the tree with the cat, not knowing how to get down." Nicholas laughed hard.

"The next thing I remember, Luca slipped and fell, and the loop in his jeans got caught, actually saving his life, stopping him from falling all the way down. But he was so skinny back then, he started to fall out of his pants! I swear to God! He was swinging his arms all over the place, and trying to keep his pants on at the same time."

Nicholas was so hysterical that Luca had to cut in to finish the story. "My pants eventually slipped all the way to my knees. I was hanging there, naked and scared for my life. And then my father came home from his trip. He was cussing me out for being so stupid, and I just hung there with my hands over my privates trying not to die."

Emery giggled.

"Finally, Nicholas and my dad brought over a ladder to help get me down. But Nicholas will never let me forget it."

Nicholas wiped the tears from his eyes as he sputtered, "He was just hanging there, with his little weenie hanging out." Nicholas's face looked like a plump tomato.

Emery giggled into her soup while Luca gave Nicholas the most appalling look.

"Little weenie?" Luca said, aghast. "I was eight!" He clubbed his cousin in the arm.

"Boys, calm down now," Maria snapped.

They all sat in comfortable silence, eating their soup. Emery found herself staring at Luca's mouth, unearthing a feeling inside her that she couldn't describe. The way his lips moved while he chewed was oddly erotic. The dimples in his cheeks appeared, and her heart nearly came to a full stop.

She was in big trouble.

Shaking off her thoughts, she tried focusing on her soup.

"I have something I need to tell you, Luca," Maria said, breaking the silence.

"What?"

"It's about Pablo."

"Your brother?" Luca asked.

"Sí. I know you didn't know him that well, but you should know that he passed away a few months ago," she said. Her voice shook as she spoke. "May he rest in peace." Her hand made the sign of the cross at her head, heart, and shoulders.

"I am so sorry to hear," Luca said, putting down his spoon. The room got quiet as Maria gathered her emotions.

"There was a problem with his lungs. They kept filling with fluid. He was hospitalized twice, and they could never figure out what was causing it. But then, another guy had the same problem. Another coffee farmer."

"Was it just a coincidence?" Luca asked.

"That's no coincidence," Nicholas said. "I heard just yesterday of a third case of the same thing in Bogota. Died of some sort of lung complication they couldn't diagnose."

"What do you think it could be?" Emery asked.

"No one knows for sure, but it's only a matter of time before they can get to the bottom of it."

"I am so sorry to hear this news," Emery said sadly into her soup.

"No, I'm sorry to bring the house down," Maria said, wiping her eyes. "At least Raphael isn't here. I don't think I would have had the nerve to get all that off my chest in front of him."

Nicholas and Luca froze, holding their spoons in midair.

Emery furrowed her brow. "Why would Raphael be here?" she asked.

"Luca's brother is family, but that man is not in his right mind. He is a walking, drinking, emotional roller coaster. It's better that he stays at home."

Nicholas dropped his head in his hands.

"Raphael is your brother?" Emery asked, turning to Luca. The memory of Raphael's groin pressed against her caused her to flinch. A lump formed in the back of her throat. Setting down her napkin, she stood slowly from the table. "If you'll excuse me for a moment, I need some fresh air," she said calmly, masking the heated fury that boiled inside.

"Emery." Luca stood, walking after her through the front door. Emery quickened her pace, but Luca closed in on her arm. "Emery, please listen."

"Don't touch me!" Emery shrugged off his hand. "You lied to me!"

"Emery, por favor. I couldn't tell you."

Emery pulled away and stormed off again. Luca grabbed her arms and pulled her to face him. "Emery," he pleaded. "Listen to me." His strong hands stopped Emery in her tracks, and she locked on to his eyes.

"I didn't tell you at first because I was trying to protect you *and* him. I didn't want you to turn him in to the police. His mood swings and his drinking has gotten out of control. I couldn't let him go to jail. He needs help."

Emery stood her ground, shrugging his hands off her arms. "You could have just told me that from the beginning! You didn't have to lie to me all this time. How do I know you and Raphael weren't working together? How can I trust you now?" Heat crept up her face as she buried her tears deep down.

"You have to trust me. I came to talk to you alone. My brother was supposed to stay at home and take care of the office. I had no idea he was going to show up and try to hurt you. He is unwell. He's not right in the head. I will take care of him when I get home."

Luca got down on his knees and wrapped his arms around her waist, pressing his head against her chest. He looked up at her with the saddest puppy-dog eyes she had ever seen.

"Por favor. Believe me. Trust me," he said into the cotton fabric of her dress.

Emery stood there, motionless.

"Conejita," he pleaded.

"I need time to think," Emery said, looking away, avoiding the temptation to give in.

Luca loosened his grip on her and stood. The dampness of the ground had stained his jeans at his knees. He brushed off the grass before rubbing the back of his neck.

"Lo siento, Emery. I will never lie to you again," he said, lightly brushing his hand along the side of her cheek.

Emery resisted the urge to lean into him, and she backed away. Luca's hand froze in midair as Emery made the walk back up to the farmhouse.

When Emery and Luca walked in, Maria and Nicholas were cleaning up the kitchen. They both stopped when they saw Emery.

"Emery, I'm so sorry. I didn't realize …" Maria started.

"It is quite all right. I'm glad I know now."

"I assume you two made up?" she asked, looking at Luca, who was standing in the corner. "Why don't you both run along and head into town? There is a festival there tonight."

"I'm not sure that's a good idea," Emery said.

"Let me take you there," Luca urged.

Emery wasn't in the mood to go out, but she wasn't in the mood to stay in and sulk with Luca in the same room either. She looked up at Luca, who had been waiting patiently for an answer.

"Sure," she said finally. "I could use the distraction."

Chapter 18

I t was a long, silent truck ride into town. Emery didn't say a word. She wouldn't even look him in the eye.

Luca parked his truck on the street near a terracotta church with two giant domes overlooking a square full of people. A Colombian band played music on a stage covered by a large white tent. People danced in the square, surrounded by street vendors selling food out of their carts. Children ran between dancing couples and families sitting down to eat, watching the festival.

Emery looked mesmerized by the sights and the sounds of the town square. Her blue dress flapped in the wind. She held down her hair with one hand while she shielded her eyes from the beating sun with the other.

Luca walked over to her and held out his hand. Emery glanced at it but walked on, leaving his hand hanging in the air. He closed his fist, gathering his patience as he followed her toward the square.

It was hard to tell from behind, but as she walked a few paces ahead of him, it appeared she might have been smiling at the townspeople as they welcomed her onto the patio.

Perhaps she was lightening up.

He stood back and watched her approach the musicians.

Her hips swayed to the beat of the drums, and the singer made eye contact with her, giving her a wink. When she turned around, Luca saw her smiling, that is, until she caught Luca's gaze. Her smile faded instantaneously, and she walked off the patio toward the plastic tables and chairs. Crossing her legs, she turned her back to Luca and watched the happy, dancing villagers.

So that's how it's going to be?

He prowled toward her, walking menacingly slow. As if she could feel the heat from him, she turned to look up just as he offered his hand to the girl sitting next to her. The girl was young, possibly in her early twenties. Her low-cut tank top left very little to the imagination. The girl blushed at first but then accepted Luca's hand. He led her onto the patio and looked back quickly to find Emery in a simmering pool of rage.

Bueno.

Luca twirled the young girl around the dance floor and swayed his hips with the beat. She wrapped her arms around his neck and followed him with every move. Her shiny hair flowed from side to side, swaying to the sound of the music.

At the edge of the dance floor, Emery was accepting a hand from one of the locals wearing a cowboy hat and a black V-neck shirt. Emery sent daggers through her eyes back at Luca as she walked toward the dance floor with the greasy weasel at her hand.

The young girl in Luca's arms looked behind her to see what had caught Luca's attention. She turned back and frowned.

"Lo siento," Luca said as he walked her back to her seat. She sat down in a huff, but Luca didn't care. He made a beeline to the dead man with the hand on Emery's lower back. He stood next to him until the weasel accidentally bumped into Luca's chest.

The man looked up at Luca, who was a good six inches taller than him. Luca sent him a death glare, and the man threw his hands up in surrender. Luca shoved him aside and grabbed Emery as if she were his to possess.

"Hey!" Emery called, squirming under his hold.

He dipped down toward her ear and whispered softly, but firmly. "I don't ever want to see you in the arms of another man again."

Emery looked up at him, stunned and speechless. Her breath became heavy on his neck, and her pulse quickened through her palms. They stared at each other in intense silence until the music kicked on again.

Rising up to Luca's ear, Emery whispered back. "You ever strongarm me again, I'll rip those dimples off your face and eat them for breakfast."

Luca's eyebrows shot up and he loosened his grip on her, noting how she didn't leave. Instead, she smiled. Her stony exterior crumbled before his eyes, and relief settled into his chest.

The beat of the drums inspired him to move to the music. Emery looked down and shook her head.

"Come on. Dance with me," Luca said, putting his hands on her hips. She didn't back away. Pulling and pushing, his hands guided her hips to mimic his movements.

It appeared Emery felt the rhythm enough to move to the music. She laughed at herself at first, which made Luca smile. They continued to dance, bumping into other couples and twirling around with reckless abandon. Emery's carefree, fun-loving spirit was back.

Thank God. His heart couldn't have taken it any longer.

The music stopped and the crowd clapped, including Emery and Luca. Heat had built between them, and Luca's chest rose and fell as he normalized his breath. Emery's cheeks had a rosy glow, and the wispy hairs that framed her face clung to her damp skin.

A slow, romantic melody played on a guitar had begun, and a woman wearing a blue and gold ruffled dress took the mic and sang a sweet Colombian song. Her voice was low and seductive.

Luca looked down at Emery's sparkling hazel eyes and hummed to the melody of the music. He pulled her close, clasped his hands around hers, and began to dance. Emery closed her eyes and melted into his chest. She felt so good in his arms. Soft and delicate. Like a precious flower he had to protect.

They swayed gently to the music together until a raindrop hit Luca's nose. They both looked up. Heavy clouds had rolled in.

Luca looked down and found more raindrops falling from the sky.

The music picked up to a tropical beat, and Luca twirled Emery around, letting her skirt fan out around her. She laughed as he brought her back into his grasp and continued to rock his hips with hers.

Luca looked down at Emery's mouth. Her lips were glistening. Wet from the rain. She parted her lips, as if drawing him into her. Luca couldn't restrain himself anymore, and he took her mouth with his, tasting the rain and the sweetness of her tongue.

God, she tasted so good.

The pent-up desire radiated through Luca's veins as she

kissed him back, giving him everything in return. She slipped her tongue against his and he felt himself losing control. He tightened his arms around her while the rain began to pour.

Her dress had become soaked from the harsh rain. Luca let go of their kiss and looked at Emery's dazed face as she tried to flutter her eyes open.

"We need to go."

People had scattered from the town square, running for cover under tents and awnings.

Luca grabbed Emery's hand, and they ran across the street to an open cafe. Emery was drenching wet, her hair dripping on the ground under the canopy. She wrung out her hair onto the sidewalk and laughed at how soaked they had gotten. Her wet dress clung to the contours of her body and her nipples poked through the damp fabric.

He pulled her in close to prevent others from getting a glimpse as they walked into the cafe.

"Que pasa?" said the man at the counter. "Can I get you anything?"

"Dos cafes, por favor. Can we use your bathroom to clean up?" Luca asked, clutching Emery to his side.

Luca opened the bathroom and locked the door behind him. Emery walked to the mirror and saw that her dress had clung to her body, becoming embarrassingly revealing.

"Oh my God. I'm practically naked!" she shrieked in the mirror. She quickly covered her breasts and looked at Luca as he laughed in the back corner.

"It's not funny!" she laughed, playfully hitting his shoulder. "I am so embarrassed!"

They laughed together as she wrung out her dress into the sink while trying not to expose herself any more.

Luca's laugh grew even stronger as the water poured from her skirt.

"This is useless," she said, wringing out the very last drop and letting her wet dress fall back into place. "I look like a sopping wet mess with tits."

"You look more beautiful now than you did at the gala," Luca said, walking toward her. He slowly backed her up to the bathroom door, placing both hands on either side of her face. He pressed into her and claimed her mouth.

Emery wrapped her leg around his waist as he pinned her against the door. She dug her fingers into his back, pulling him closer.

Luca's hands drew down her spine and around her behind. He wanted to feel every inch of her. His hands continued to roam down her hips and up toward her breasts.

"I want you," Emery said breathlessly.

Luca found himself paralyzed by the sound of those three simple words. He bathed himself in the heat of her stare before plunging into her mouth again. His hands glided up her legs, finding the lace of her underwear.

Knock, knock, knock.

"Hola?" a man called out from behind the door.

"Christ," Luca sighed.

Emery giggled into his mouth.

"Un momento, por favor," Luca shouted, giving Emery one last punishing kiss before he stepped back. He gave himself a few calming breaths with his hands on his hips.

"Let's take our coffees to go."

***

Rain pounded on the truck windshield as they made their way back to the farm. Reflections of water droplets covered Luca's face. As they pulled in front of the horses' stables, Emery watched his perfect lips form into a smile.

Luca got out of the truck and ran to the passenger side, rain drenching his clothes while he opened the door. Emery huddled under his arm as he tried to shield her from the downpour. Together they made the climb up the stairs to the small studio above the stables.

Luca was soaked from head to toe, his hair dripping water on the floor. He pulled off his sopping shirt and squeezed it into the sink across the room. His powerful back was on full display. A stirring deep in her core emerged as she watched his muscles ripple while he wrung out his shirt.

The pitter-patter of droplets at her feet made Emery look down. She had left a puddle on the floor. She carefully stepped out of her shoes and peeled off her dress, shyly covering herself as she approached the sink. Pretending she couldn't feel his arm touching hers, she wrung out her dress and caught Luca eyeing her lacy bra through the mirror.

When she looked up, she could see the desperate hunger in his eyes. He wet his lips, watching her as she hung her dress on the hook next to the sink. He stepped forward, closing the distance between them, and reached over to hang his shirt on the hook next to her dress. His arm lightly grazed the top of Emery's shoulder, sending shivers up her neck.

They stood, facing each other like the calm before the storm, until they lunged at each other, their mouths and bodies joined in a fury of passion. Luca pinned Emery's arms and pressed her back against the window. The window was cold, and the sill dug into her hip, but she immersed herself in the heat of his chest and the softness of his lips. Luca lifted her legs around his waist, and he leaned into her. Emery drew in a sharp breath as his desire pushed between her legs.

The rain pounded on the window and echoed in the room. Emery's breath grew stronger and louder as Luca pressed his body into hers. He grabbed her waist, lifting her up off the floor and carrying her to the bed. He laid her down with such force that Emery bounced up from the springy bed, knocking their foreheads together.

"Ouch!" Emery cupped her head in pain.

"Lo siento, did I hurt you?" Luca asked, rubbing his forehead.

Emery shook her head, and they both laughed before lunging at each other again. Emery explored his broad back with her hands and tugged at his jeans until they fell on the floor, like a present being unwrapped on Christmas Day. Emery smoothed her hands over his caramel chest and stomach, feeling the soft curls just below his belly button.

Luca slipped his fingers around her panties and slowly pulled them down her thighs, not letting an inch of her skin go untouched. His mouth found its way from her navel to her breasts. Emery moaned with pleasure, tilting her hips to meet his, and their bodies became one.

Under the beating of raindrops on the tin roof above, Emery found a passion she had never experienced before, concluding with delicious waves of trembling explosions.

Emery lay next to Luca with inexplicable tears at the corners of her eyes. Her world completely turned upside down and inside out.

"Are you still with me, conejita?" Luca brushed the hair out of her face, planting a kiss on her forehead.

"Yes, but I feel like I left Earth for a moment there."

"That's why I asked," Luca said with a smile. "I'm glad you're back."

Chapter 19

The office was in disarray. Papers were thrown about, and the blinking red light on the answering machine indicated there were twelve missed calls. Raphael stormed to the back and found Juan and Mateo working with a small crew of men, washing the coffee beans.

"Where's Fernando?"

"I'm not sure. He wasn't in his room this morning," Juan said.

Raphael flared his nostrils. He tore down the gravel path to Luca's house and screamed at the top of his lungs.

"Fernando!"

The front door was unlocked. Like an animal, he prowled through the living room looking for signs of life. He walked down the hall to the bedroom and opened the door to find Luisa Santiago wrapped in a bedsheet, hovering over his son's body. She was frantically trying to put clothes on Fernando. Blood covered the pillowcase and his face.

"What did you do?" Raphael grabbed Luisa and tossed her across the room. The loud thud of her head hitting the bedroom wall didn't even register as he cowered over his son's lifeless body.

"He passed out," Luisa cried, tears streaming down her face.

She could hardly get the words out. "He was coughing up blood. We have to get him to the hospital."

Raphael turned toward Luisa. She was sniffling in the corner of the room, like a scared little mouse.

"Get out of this house," Raphael snapped. "Now!"

Luisa's face was red-hot, and she stood there blubbering, paralyzed and terrified.

"I said *get out*!" Raphael barked. He picked up what looked like her clothes from the floor and threw them at her face. She struggled to hold the sheet up and scrambled out of the room in hysterics.

Fernando's handsome face had turned pale, his body limp like a ragdoll, completely helpless.

"My boy," Raphael put his arm around Fernando to pull him up. He grunted, throwing all his strength and weight forward, carrying Fernando through the house and out the door. Step by step, he dragged his son across the gravel path, Fernando's weight punishing Raphael's lower back and knees. The peaceful sounds that normally decorated the fields were replaced by the heaving sound of his breath. He finally reached his truck, and it took every ounce of his power to place Fernando's limp body in the back seat before tearing down the dusty road.

Chapter 20

Maria stood over the stove, scrambling a batch of eggs, her hips bouncing vigorously as she whisked her spatula around and around the pan.

"Buenos días, Maria."

"Luca! Good morning, dear. Did you and Emery work things out last night?"

"Uh, sí. Everything is fine now." He couldn't help grinning from ear to ear.

"Ah, I see. You really like this one, no?" she said, shaking her spatula at him.

"Sí." Luca closed his eyes and let out the breath he was holding in. "I really do."

"Thank God," she said as she looked up at the ceiling. She walked over to give Luca a warm hug. "I can tell she likes you too. Here, take some food with you back to the loft. You two must be hungry," she said, fixing a plate.

Luca walked out of the farmhouse carrying a carafe of coffee and a covered plate. The morning sun greeted him with warm kisses on his nose and cheeks, and a symphony of birds chirped sweet love songs as he made the walk back to the stables.

Luca winced at the creaking sound of rotted floorboards underfoot. He hoped not to disturb Emery in case she was still asleep. As he peeked behind the bedroom door, he found Emery bolted upright in bed, her hair matted on one side of her head and a wildly tangled forest on the other side. She squinted as her eyes adjusted to the morning light that burst through the bedroom door.

"Buenos días, conejita."

Emery grunted under her breath while Luca poured the coffee. She sounded like an angry cavewoman.

"Grumble, grumble. Mer mer."

Was she talking or growling at him?

"Qué?" he asked, handing her a cup. She sipped slowly. A moment later her eyes brightened, and color came back to her cheeks. A smile formed as she straightened her posture. Emery clutched her coffee to her chest. "Thank you. You are a saint."

"I see a little bit of coffee goes a long way with you." He smirked, pouring himself a cup.

"Yes," Emery purred, taking another sip. "And you brought breakfast in bed too? Wow, I feel spoiled."

"You need the strength so that I can ravish you in bed again."

Emery nearly choked on her coffee.

Luca smiled as he stabbed some eggs with his fork and brought them to Emery's mouth.

"Eat."

Emery opened her mouth, letting Luca place the eggs delicately on her tongue. He squirmed next to her, waiting impatiently to touch her again.

Emery hummed with delight as she chewed, and Luca couldn't handle the tease anymore.

"If you keep making noises like that, I may need to throw the food away out of jealousy."

"How could you think of doing something so barbaric." Emery swallowed her bite. "To the most delicious eggs I have ever tasted."

Luca laughed and took a bite of his own.

"These are definitely good. I suppose I can wait."

Luca watched Emery as she drank her coffee, smiling at how cute she looked with her hair in disarray.

"What's so funny?" she asked, taking another sip of his coffee.

"Your hair," he teased.

"*My* hair? Now that's funny. Have you not seen yours yet?" she asked, pointing toward the mirror in the main room.

They both got up together and looked at each other in the mirror. Luca's hair was every bit as wild as hers. They laughed together, trying to pat down each other's wild manes to no avail. Eventually, they gave up and got back in bed, giggling into their coffees and eggs until their bellies ached.

***

Jake walked into the lobby of the Medellín office with Esmeralda following close behind. The floors were covered in marble tiles, adorned with planted palms and birds of paradise around the grand lobby. A vaulted ceiling with glass windows arched over the room, letting the natural light cascade over the bustling first floor.

Esmeralda caught her reflection in the glass door and stopped to pull and shape the top half of her dress, squeezing her breasts together as she adjusted her cleavage. She pouted her lips together and fluffed her hair before balancing her way through the double doors in her tight-fitted black dress and three-inch heels, oblivious to the stares she was getting as men and women in business suits shuffled past them to catch the next elevator ride.

This was a bad idea, Jake thought to himself as he handed over his ID to the receptionist. The lady at the desk typed something in the computer and then handed over the ID with a visitor badge.

"I'll need an ID for your *friend* as well."

Esmeralda shuffled through her purse, pulling out tubes of lipstick and mascara and placing them on the desk. Compact cases, tampons, lotions, and nail files soon cluttered the counter. Jake rubbed his temples as the growing sense of regret combined forces with his head-splitting hangover.

"Ah ha!" she exclaimed, handing it to the receptionist.

"The Coffee Benz offices are on the sixth floor. Take the elevators to your right, and use your badges to get through security."

"Gracias." Jake smiled. He took Esmeralda's hand and weaved in and out through the professional businesspeople walking across the first floor.

On the sixth floor, Jake found a quiet, empty office and immediately sat down at the desk. He opened his briefcase and pulled out his phone book, flipping through it to find Don Campbell's number.

"Don Campbell's office, how can I help you?" said the woman's voice on the other line.

"Sheila, it's Jake Whitmore. Can you put me through to Don? It's urgent."

"Connecting you now." The phone clicked, and a moment later Don's voice was on the other end. "Hello? Jake? Where's Emery? She was supposed to have called me by now."

"Uh, Don. It's a bit complicated at the moment. Emery is

indisposed, but everything is fine."

The silence on the other line grew heavier by the second.

"We hit a few unanticipated challenges down here," Jake said, running his hand through his hair. "I don't think we'll be able to—"

"Nonsense. Jake, I've sent Emery down there to cut our costs. If Emery can't get it done, then we'll have to reposition her in the company to do something else."

"Don, I'm telling you there are complications to us being here right now. Let us gather some of the facts while we're here, and I'll send you a recap."

"I'm not liking the sound of this one bit, Whitmore. Either you come back with lowered rates, or else we'll have to find replacements for the both of you."

"Don—"

Click.

Jake put his head in his hands and let out an aggravated sigh. A moment later, Esmeralda placed her hand on his shoulder. He gazed into Esmeralda's worried eyes.

"Que pasa?" she asked.

Jake shook his head. He didn't have the energy to explain, or to think of a plan.

"You know, I just remembered that Luca has a cousin who owns a farm not too far away. I don't know his name, but we can call around to see if any of these farmers are related to Luca."

"Brilliant!" Jake cried, grabbing her face and kissing her on the mouth. He picked up the phone and dialed another phone number.

"Jeanine? Hey, it's me, Jake. Can you get me a list of all the Colombian coffee farms we work with within an hour of

Medellín?"

"Hey, sweetie. Sure, I can," Jeanine said on the other line. "Where's Emery?"

"She's indisposed at the moment. We're doing a little bit of a tour of Colombia and wanted to get a good sampling of the farms we work with."

"I see. All right, where should I send the list?"

"Go ahead and fax it over to the Medellín office. Thanks."

Jake hung up, grinning widely.

Moments later, a fax arrived with a list of names and addresses. Jake and Esmeralda looked over the list together. There had to have been over twenty farms. "We'll never find them."

"We will," Esmeralda said, a determined spark in her voice. "We will definitely find them."

Chapter 21

The birds chirped in the background as Emery lay in Luca's arms, snuggled together under the covers of the twin-size bed. He caressed the top of her shoulder and followed her silky skin down to the bony point of her elbow.

Emery's thoughts marched through the crease in her forehead. He knew that he was losing time with her. She needed to go back, but he wanted to hold on to her forever.

Maybe he could convince her to stay and help him run the farm? Or perhaps she could get a job with the Coffee Federation in Medellín and they could see each other on weekends. Would she be happy here?

Luca opened his mouth to ask but was interrupted by the door.

"Knock, knock. Hola! It's Maria!" Maria barged in, startling Emery. She shifted below the covers and sank into her pillow, her face flushed a deep red.

"Sorry to barge in," Maria said, averting her eyes.

"No, you're not." Luca smiled. "What can we do for you, Maria?"

"I was wondering if you could run to town and pick up a few things for me? I have so much work to do here, I could use a hand."

"Sure, no problem," Luca said. "I can head to town before I take Emery back to the city."

"I hate to see you go, Emery," Maria said with a frown.

Emery looked up at Luca, her eyes swimming in the same sadness that tugged at Luca's heart. "I'm sad to go," Emery said.

"Please stop by the house before you head out, okay, darling? And thank you, Luca. I just need a large bag of fertilizer for the vegetable garden. Our tomatoes are looking a little malnourished." She blew each of them a kiss before backing out of the door. "Gracias!"

Luca looked down at Emery to find a tear rolling down her cheek.

"What's wrong, conejita?" He brought her back to his chest and caressed her hair as she nestled into his neck.

"I guess I'm just sad at the thought of saying goodbye," she said as her tear dropped onto his chest. The tear touched Luca's skin, making ripples on his soul.

"You don't have to go, you know."

"How do you mean?"

"I mean, you could stay in Colombia. Help me with the farm, maybe? Work in Medellín? Or you could stay in my bed all day, and I'll feed you and take care of you for the rest of time."

Luca could see the ping-pong effect of her thoughts all over her face. He understood it was a lot to ask, but part of him wished it would have been an easy decision for her.

"You don't need to decide right now," he said, giving her a squeeze.

Emery let out an audible sigh of relief.

"How about this: I'll head to town to get Maria her bag of poop," he said with a mischievous smile. "You stay in bed and think about it. I'll be back in a little while."

"I can come with you if you want," she said.

"You rest here. There's a shower around the back if you want to use it. I'll be back before you know it."

He bent down and gave her a kiss on her forehead.

***

Maria lay in bed that morning, looking at the empty spot next to her. Nicholas must have already left for town. She pursed her eyebrows together. *Darn.* She forgot to ask him to pick up fertilizer on the way home.

She pulled the covers off her legs and stepped onto the cool wooden floor. Her nightgown tickled the tops of her bare feet as she walked over to the kitchen. Her eyes squinted, adjusting to the light pouring in from the window as she began to make a pot of coffee.

She cracked an egg into the frying pan, and a sizzling sound filled the room. Maria hummed to herself as she added a few more eggs for the two little lovebirds above the stables. She smiled to herself, thinking of how Luca was looking at Emery yesterday. He was smitten. And she obviously had feelings for him in return. *They would be such a beautiful couple,* Maria thought. She chuckled at the idea. Luca had been a ladies' man, tossing women aside pretty quickly. Never getting attached. Nobody thought he would ever settle down. Perhaps this girl was different. Emery was not like the other girls he's been seen with before. Emery had class. She was sophisticated. A stark contrast to the ladies that seemed to be knocking on Luca's door.

The phone rang, interrupting Maria's thoughts.

Maria picked up the phone. "Hola?"

"Hello, is this Nicholas Garcia's residence?" said the American voice on the other end.

"Sí. And who is this?"

"Hi, My name is…Carl, and I am a friend of Luca Mendoza. Any chance you know him?"

"Sí, is everything okay?"

"He dropped his credit card at a tavern in Medellín. I was trying to find a way to get it to him, but he isn't at home. Is he with you by chance?" the man asked.

"Oh my, that is so kind of you. Yes, he is here, but he will be heading back to—"

Click.

"Hola?"

The call had been disconnected. *That was strange*, Maria thought as she got back to her eggs.

Chapter 22

Luca walked out of the store with the heavy bag of fertilizer, and a flash of light caught his eye. Across the street was a flea market with tables full of trinkets and jewelry. An old woman with long white hair and tan leathery skin sat at a table with hand-carved wooden sculptures. Around her neck dangled a beaded pendant, catching the sunlight and ricocheting it into Luca's eyes.

Luca moved out of the way from the offending reflection. The old woman was looking directly at him, gesturing for him to come to the table. Luca plopped the large bag of fertilizer into the back of the truck and made his way across the street to the old woman.

"Buenos días," the woman said. One of her eyes was a softer shade of blue than the other. She looked down at her table of figurines, but she used her hands to feel for the one she was looking for.

"Oh no, gracias. I don't need a—"

"Here," she said, finding the one she was searching for. She placed the small figurine in his palm. Her wrinkly fingers wrapped around his hands, and she squeezed. She looked up at him, but her eyes could not fixate on one thing. Her light blue iris sparkled in the light, while the other bore a hole through his forehead.

"I want you to have this," she said, giving him a squeeze. "And never let go."

"That's really nice of you, but I can't accept it."

Luca opened his hands to find a carved wooden rabbit with a delicate engraved floral pattern along its back. A beautiful conejita. He stared at it long and hard, his jaw agape.

"How?"

The old woman shook her head as she reached for her cane and sat in her chair.

"This is perfect. In every way. Gracias, mucho."

Luca reached for his back pocket, but the old woman swatted at his arm.

"Consider it a present from my dreams. Now you must go…" The woman pointed at Luca's truck. "Before it's too late."

"Too late for what?"

"Go!" she screeched.

Luca startled at the woman's abrupt change in demeanor and backed away slowly.

What a peculiar woman, he thought. He ran his thumb over the grooves of the wooden figurine, looking over the sweet little rabbit face and adorable pinned-back ears. Emery was going to love this. He smiled, but the old woman's warning etched in the back of his mind, pestering him all the way back to the farm.

Chapter 23

T he four-door rental car hobbled over the gravel road, catching the attention of the coffee farmers in white sun hats tending to their harvest. They stared at Jake and Esmeralda as if they had disturbed their peace with the coffee trees.

Jake's palms sweated underneath the steering wheel. His anxiety grew with every pothole between entrance and the Garcia Coffee Farm. Would Emery believe him if he told her Luca was using her? Or was it too late? Had she fallen in love with him?

Esmeralda pressed her lips together and puckered her mouth in the mirror. Her eyelashes had doubled in size since he had last looked over at her.

"You nervous or something?" Esmeralda asked aloud without taking her eyes off herself in the mirror.

"No," Jake lied. He slowly pulled up to a stable. A woman wearing a bright blue dress was petting one of the horses. As Jake got a closer look, he realized it was Emery.

"Emery!" He shifted the car into park.

"Stay here," Jake said firmly to Esmeralda as she squinted toward the stables.

Emery put her hand above her eyes to shield the sun and

took a few steps forward. She looked a little confused, but more importantly, she looked alone. Jake opened the car door and stepped onto the damp earth, the mud splattering on his oxfords.

"Shit," he said, looking down at his soiled shoes.

"Jake?"

"Emery! I've been looking all over for you," Jake said, shaking off his muddy shoe situation and walking to her with open arms. She walked up to him for a brief hug, but then looked behind him toward the car.

"Who's with you?" she asked. "And how did you find me? I left you a message at the hotel to say that I was all right. We were going to head back today—"

"Is Luca here?"

"He went to the store. Why?"

"Listen to me. You need to leave here now."

"Leave now? What are you talking about?"

Jake looked around and let out a large sigh before he could begin.

"Luca has been using you to save his farm."

"What do you mean?"

"This whole thing was his master plan. He was going to take you back to the farm, seduce you, and change your mind about the negotiations. I know because his brother told me."

"Raphael told you that?"

"Yes."

Emery shook her head in denial. "No, that can't be."

"He's playing you, Emery. Just like he played the woman with the peacock feather at the bar. Remember her? I found out that he had seduced her, tricking her into letting him into the gala the other night. He never had an invitation."

"I can't believe this is true."

"I'm so sorry, Em." He reached for her, but she shrugged him off.

Emery's face grew pale. She feverishly shook her head, her hands in her hair. Tears welled in her eyes as she kept repeating, "I can't believe it. I can't believe it."

A car door slammed, and Jake's head jerked back. Esmeralda made her way in her high heels toward them, a scowl on her face as her breasts bounced through the tough terrain.

"So this is the bitch who's been sleeping with my Luca?" Esmeralda shouted.

"*Your* Luca?" Emery gasped.

"Esmeralda, go back to the car," Jake said angrily, but Esmeralda charged toward them.

"You listen here, bitch," Esmeralda said as she struggled to get past Jake's grasp. Jake tried holding her in place, but she was like an animal, a wildcat about to pounce on her prey. "Luca isn't going to settle for some straight-laced, boring white girl like you. He needs a real woman, like me. He is mine!"

Jake couldn't believe what he was hearing. He struggled to contain her as she thrashed about.

"Esmeralda, what about us?" he whispered in her ear.

"I told you from the beginning that you're not my type," she snapped back, pushing herself away from him.

"You used me?"

"Sorry, honey," she said, looking at her manicure. "Now take your pathetic little white girl back to Boring Town, and leave my man to me," she said, stomping her foot on the ground. The oozing sound of mud had Jake both stunned and disgusted.

"I'll get my things and we can go," Emery said, defeatedly walking toward the stairs.

Jake looked back at Esmeralda. She had a victorious look on her face, her arms crossed as she tapped her toe, waiting impatiently for Emery and Jake to leave.

Emery came back down the stairs with a grocery bag full of what looked to be a crumpled evening gown. She looked ill, walking past Jake and Esmeralda as if she did not see them anymore.

Jake followed behind her, watching her struggle through the muddy terrain.

"Thanks for the ride, white boy," Esmeralda called as she hobbled toward the stables.

"Whore," Jake said, shaking his head and turning back toward the car.

Emery stopped to look at the farmhouse up the gravel road.

"Are you okay?" he asked.

"Let's just go," she said as she opened the car door and slumped in the passenger seat.

***

Luca rubbed the wooden rabbit figurine with his thumb as he hopped up the steps above the stable. Smiling to himself, he thought about what Emery's reaction would be when she saw it. Even if she might not be ready to leave her home just yet and come live with him in Colombia, she would at least have something to take back with her. To remember him by.

The door creaked open, and the living room was quiet. He walked to the bedroom door, pushing it open, his brain playing tricks on him. He was expecting to find Emery resting in bed, her auburn hair flowing across her freckled skin, but instead, he was faced with hair as dark as night and lips as red as blood.

Esmeralda.

"What are you doing here? Where is Emery?" he growled.

"She left with the white boy," Esmeralda said, fidgeting with her nails.

"What did you do?" Luca said in a low voice.

"Honestly, I don't know what you saw in her, but I forgive you. Emery left with Jake the moment she saw him. It was obvious she was eager to go home."

"You're lying."

"I think I even heard her say something like, *Oh, Jake, I've missed you so much. Please get me away from here. I've been kidnapped.* Or something like that."

Luca grabbed Esmeralda by the arm, jolting her from her reclined position on the bed.

"Tell me where she is!"

"Honey, don't worry about her anymore. She's nothing. You have me now." Esmeralda ignored the grip Luca had on her left arm, and she trailed her long red fingernail up his arm. Her touch repulsed him. He shrugged her off, leaving her in his wake as he bounded to the door.

"Wait, Luca. Where are you going?" The whiny voice came from the top of the stairs.

Luca froze before getting into his truck. He couldn't just leave Esmeralda here. He didn't want to put the burden on Maria to take out the trash.

"Get in the truck," he snarled.

Esmeralda pouted all the way down the stairs and tip-toed through the muddy ground in her heels, her hips sashaying from side to side. Luca's patience had grown so thin, he nearly burst when Esmeralda flopped into the passenger seat and crossed her arms.

"Where are we going?"

Luca pulled the truck into reverse and drove into town in determined silence.

They approached an old gas station with only one pump. An old man wearing a cowboy hat and a toothless smile stood up from his seat when Luca hopped out of the truck.

"Does the bus line to Medellín come through here at this stop?" Luca asked.

The old man nodded, pointing to the yellowed bus schedule hung with scotch tape behind the gas station window.

"I'll take one bus ticket, please," Luca said, handing over a few pesos. The clerk scuffed his way inside the shop and came out with a bus ticket.

Esmeralda got out of the truck and slammed the door behind her.

"What's going on?" she asked, her hands in the air, wobbling on her three-inch heels.

Luca approached her, handing her a ticket stub.

"There's a bus coming in fifteen minutes that will bring you back to Medellín."

"But I don't want to go back to Medellín. I want to come home with you." She stomped her foot like a toddler, sticking out her bottom lip.

"Listen to me carefully. I don't know what you did or said to Emery. But I do know that I never want to see you again. Take the bus, or not. You're not coming with me."

"But—"

Luca turned his back to her as he walked toward the truck.

"Luca! Don't do this to me! Luca! You can't leave me here! I love you—"

Slam. The door shut before he could hear another word.

Revving the engine, he put his car into drive, peeling his car around the gas station pump, leaving a dust cloud trail behind him.

Esmeralda's abandoned purse sat on the passenger seat of his car. In one swift motion, he grabbed it with his right hand and threw it out the window, where it landed near Esmeralda's feet. Makeup and bottles of who-knew-what flew out of the purse and scattered across the ground.

Chapter 24

Luca pulled his truck into the valet parking of the Hotel du Park Royal. A valet boy wearing a red and black jacket with yellow piping along the sleeves approached him. Luca tossed his keys to the boy, letting them jingle all the way to the ground. Luca had already left him behind, sprinting to the hotel concierge.

"Buenos días," the concierge aid. "How can I help you?"

"Emerson Smith, por favor." Luca gasped, catching his breath. "Can you please let her know that Luca Mendoza is here?"

The concierge typed into the keyboard and dialed a number on the phone.

Luca paced back and forth, his hands on his hips. He wasn't sure what Esmeralda or Jake had told her, but whatever it was, it must have been bad. So bad that Emery was willing to leave without saying goodbye. There was no conceivable reason in his mind that Emery would leap into Jake's arms and beg him to take her back to the city.

He bit his lip nervously as the concierge spoke softly on the phone.

"I see." The concierge raised her eyebrows. "Claro. I will see to it right away."

His heart pounded as he watched the concierge rest the phone back down.

"I am sorry, but Señorita Smith is not taking visitors at this time."

The words were like daggers to his heart.

"Then I'll wait here," Luca said firmly.

"Señor Mendoza, Emerson has asked politely for you to leave the hotel."

Luca eyebrows pursed together, his hands balled into fists. He slammed the receptionist desk. "I need to talk to her!"

"Señor Mendoza, you must calm down, or I will have our security escort you out immediately."

Luca's chest heaved. He stared at the receptionist, daring her to call the police. She looked past him, sending a signal to someone behind him. Luca turned around to find a security guard walking his way.

"I'm sorry," Luca said defeatedly. With slumped shoulders, he trudged to the front entrance and stepped outside, pulling a cigarette from the pack resting in his breast pocket.

His stomach ached at the thought of Emery pushing him away without giving him a chance to talk to her. There had to be a way to find her in the hotel. He just needed to figure out how to sneak past the concierge. He blew out a puff of smoke as a bellhop rolled out a large metal cart that clanked against the metal grooves of the automatic sliding doorway.

He stood at the side of the street, looking down at his watch. A minute later, a large tour bus pulled in from the busy city street and pulled up to the main entrance.

Elderly couples in floral shirts and fanny packs, cameras hanging around their necks, walked off the bus and slowly made their way into the hotel. The bellhop loaded bag after bag onto the cart, pausing to wipe the bead of sweat that formed on his brow.

Luca took one last long drag of his cigarette as he watched the last of the luggage placed on the rolling cart. The bellhop carefully rolled it toward the front doors, and Luca stomped on his cigarette butt and tossed his cowboy hat into the bushes. Following close behind the tall cart of luggage, Luca slipped past the concierge, who was busy welcoming the long line of old couples in matching Bermuda shorts.

Darting to the elevators, he slipped in as the doors closed. He looked at the buttons in complete despair. Where did he even begin? His finger hovered over the buttons until he decided to start at the top.

***

Emery calmly set the phone back on the cradle. Her anger had settled into coldhearted indifference. She convinced herself that she didn't care that he was at the hotel, but she didn't want to have anything to do with him anymore.

Everything that had ever come out of that man's mouth was a lie. He was calculating and manipulative, just as Jake had said. Emery was disappointed with herself that she didn't just trust her instincts from the beginning. Jake had warned her, but she didn't listen. Little did she realize she could be duped so easily.

Emery's head pounded. She stood and poured herself a glass of wine from the minibar and walked over to her window. People covered the sidewalks, like ants on an ant hill. The festival was over, the flowers were put away, and the music had stopped. What used to feel like a vibrant city, full of life and unexpected surprises, now felt like a hollow shell. The flower festival was merely a temporary disguise; a facade that hid the truth of what this city was really like: empty promises.

Emery took another sip of her wine when she heard heavy knocking on a door down the hall. A man was yelling, muffled by the thick hotel walls. Emery walked to the door. The knocking got louder and closer.

"Emery!" said the man's voice, calling out down the hall.

Oh no. Emery looked through the peephole in her door. A blurry image of a man was knocking on her neighbor's door.

"Emery!" Luca shouted. "Are you there?" He crumpled to the floor in front of the hotel room. The door swung open, and a large man in boxer shorts appeared, his white socks pulled over thick tree trunk legs.

"Who are you?"

"I'm looking for Emery. Auburn hair. Golden eyes."

"Good Lord. Get ahold of yourself, man. No, I haven't seen her."

Luca slumped back down on his knees as the man shut the hotel door in his face.

Emery couldn't take it anymore, and opened the door. Luca whipped around. His tortured expression melted away.

"Emery," he started, "I don't know what—"

"Stop," Emery said firmly, not liking the stirring of emotions that surfaced with Luca showing up in front of her hotel room. She tried to remain calm, but her right hand behind the door started to shake. "Was it part of your plan the whole time I've known you to take me back to the farm and convince me to stop the negotiations?"

"Sí, but—"

"Stop and let me finish," she interrupted, unsure if she could keep her steady cool much longer as the lump in her throat grew with each inhale.

"Are you sleeping with Esmeralda?" She braced herself for his response.

"I was, but let me explain."

It felt as if Emery had been punched in the stomach. She tried to remain upright, but it took every ounce of her power to stand tall.

"I don't need to hear any more. You need to go."

"Emery—"

"I will call the cops if you come anywhere near me again. Go." The lump in Emery's throat prevented her from saying more. Tears that waited patiently behind her eyes could not bear another minute and ran down her face, betraying her attempt to appear aloof.

Emery closed the door. She held her breath and watched through the peephole while Luca paced back and forth. His hands were on his hips, then flying through the air as he ranted and raved incoherently in Spanish. He stopped to punch the wall with such force, he left a hole in the sheetrock. Luca keeled over, clutching his hand into his chest.

Emery fought the urge to run to him and tend to his hand. She had to remind herself that he had betrayed her, lied to her. Used her.

She watched Luca finally come to his feet and walk away, out of sight from the peephole vantage point. She fell to her knees, no longer having the strength to keep her emotions at bay, and cried for the loss of what she had naively considered to be her first true love.

Chapter 25

Luca clutched the steering wheel despite the throbbing pain in his right hand. Spots of blood poked through broken skin at the tops of his knuckles. "Dammit," he cursed, looking in the rearview mirror as the city skyline faded behind the horizon. She was gone.

He wouldn't get to explain his side of the story to Emery. At least not tonight. Driving down the highway, the growing distance between them was burning a hole where she had left an imprint on his heart. Filling the hole was a growing sense of anger toward his brother for putting him in this mess. He needed to get to Raphael to set things straight once and for all.

At the plantation, Luca walked through the front door to find the office a mess. Unopened mail and unfiled papers covered the desk. The voice mail light was on.

"You have twelve new messages. First message—"

"Raphael!" Luca yelled over the voice mail lady. He ran outside and around the office to look for Raphael's truck, but his parking space was empty. He continued down the path to Raphael's one-story home and walked in the front door. The murmuring sound of television came from the living room, and the smell of stale microwave dinners lingered in the air.

"Hello?"

"In here," said one of the twins.

Luca walked past the kitchen. Dirty dishes had piled up in the sink and flowed onto the countertops. The trash can was filled to the brim. Crumpled wrappers had collected on the floor.

Luca huffed.

Juan and Mateo sat on the couch watching TV.

"Why is this house a mess? Where's your father?" Luca demanded.

"We tried calling the hotel, but you weren't there," Juan said. "He's at the hospital with Fernando."

"What happened?"

"It was his cough. There was blood and everything," Mateo added. "They are at the hospital. We have been waiting for Dad to come get us."

"I'll take you. Let's go now."

The boys scrambled to get their shoes and tossed their half-eaten dinners on top of the overflowing garbage on their way out.

Luca arrived at the hospital and checked in at the desk. The twins were unusually quiet, looking toward the floor. They weren't fidgeting or swatting at each other as they normally did. Luca hardly recognized them.

A few moments later, Raphael came through the double doors. His eyes were bloodshot and puffy around the lids. He shook his head, unable to use words at first. He tried composing himself and took a long steadying breath before he could speak.

"It's not looking good," he finally said. "They think the pesticides got into his lungs. They said they've had several cases of this recently."

"Is there nothing they can—"

"No."

"Can we see him?" Luca asked.

Raphael opened the hospital room door. The lights were off, and the dim light coming through the window made everything in the room look gray, including Fernando.

Fernando, who had once been a handsome and athletic young man, lay there with tubes sticking out of his nose and mouth. His skin was the color of dust, and he had dark circles around his eyes.

Luca grabbed Fernando's hand while the twins rushed to his other side.

"Hey, Nando." Luca's throat fought back the words.

Fernando blinked for a second before closing his eyes again.

"Hang in there. It's going to be okay," Luca struggled to say. Fernando squeezed Luca's hand.

"We're here now. Everything is fine."

Juan and Mateo sniffed back their tears.

"Brother. I promise we won't make fun of you and Luisa anymore, okay? Don't leave us, please," Juan struggled to say. Mateo put his arm around Juan. Their faces had become splotchy.

Luca's heart crumbled. It suffocated him. He looked over to Raphael, who had turned into stone. The shadow had taken over Raphael's spirit. He was motionless and unwilling to comfort his sons.

"Raphael," Luca whispered. "I'm sorry I hit you."

Raphael said nothing. He stood there like a post, not even blinking at the thought.

The heart monitor made a piercing high-pitched sound, and a swarm of hospital staff came in. The twins cried out as they were escorted into the hallway by one of the nurses.

Luca reached for Raphael's shoulder, but he fought back, twisting out of his arms until he crumpled onto the hallway floor. Raphael snorted loudly, sobbing on the cold, hard tile.

Juan and Mateo crouched next to their father and wept together, putting their arms around Raphael, despite the fact he was giving them nothing in return.

Luca paced back and forth for what felt like an hour. His eyes were burning, and his skin was hot. He watched as his brother finally put his arms around the twin boys, and they melted into each other until the doctor stepped out of the room.

"Doctor." Raphael shot up. "How is my boy?"

"Mr. Mendoza. I am so sorry…" The doctor paused. "We did everything we could."

It was like a punch to Luca's stomach. The doctor tried putting a hand on Raphael's shoulder, but Raphael shrugged him off. "No!" he growled and backed away, stampeding toward the double doors of the hospital exit.

"Raphael, stop!" Luca called, but it was too late. The look in his eyes said everything. He had completely snapped. Raphael disappeared behind the hospital doors, leaving his shattered sons in the hallway with no father.

Luca put his arms around his nephews and held them close. "It's okay." Luca's body shook. "It's going to be okay."

***

Luca and the twins made the defeated walk through the hospital hallway. Everything was in slow motion. His feet felt like lead. He pushed through the hospital doors to the waiting room. At the front desk, a young girl was pleading with the receptionist to be let in the hospital.

"Please. You have to let me see him," she begged.

Juan nudged Mateo to get his attention and pointed to the girl. They both looked at each other, eyebrows raised.

"Que pasa?" Luca asked the boys. "Who is that?"

"Luisa Santiago," said Juan.

"Shhhhit." Luca let out a sigh. "You boys go ahead and get in the car. I'll be right there."

Luca walked over to the young girl. Her hair was braided to the side. Her skin was blotchy from crying, but she was still pretty. Her round brown eyes looked up at Luca as he approached.

"Luisa?" Luca asked softly.

"Sí," Luisa said, drying her eyes. She looked up with so much hope that Luca's heart broke all over again for his nephew.

"Fernando? Is he okay?" she asked, clutching her tissue.

"Lo siento." Luca struggled to find the words to explain. "Fernando is in heaven with his mother now."

Luisa shook her head. "No," she whispered in disbelief. Luca opened his arms to her, and she fell into his chest, sobbing uncontrollably. Her body shook as she sputtered, "My love," over and over again.

Chapter 26

Emery stepped off the elevator of the Medellín building onto the sixth floor and shuffled down the corporate office hallway, her briefcase feeling like it weighed one hundred pounds. She walked past offices of people she should probably introduce herself to, but instead, she kept walking, looking for the empty office in the back corner of the east wing where she had been told to go.

The door to the office was slightly ajar, and a light was on. Jake sat at the desk, reading something on the computer screen when she walked in.

"Hey, boss. Here, let me give you your seat here, and I'll just move over. Are you okay? You look like you had a rough night."

"I couldn't sleep, but I'm fine," Emery said, unloading the heavy briefcase on the desk.

"The past couple days have been pretty dramatic," Jake said, sitting down in the cushioned chair across the room. His right leg crossed over his left knee, and he threw his hands behind his head like he didn't have a care in the world. Jake wouldn't have understood how dramatic it really was. How ludicrous to have fallen in love so quickly with someone who clearly had ulterior motives the entire time. She should have been up all night thinking about work, but instead, she stayed up crying over her foolish broken heart, mad at herself more than anyone else.

"Hey, I was thinking it might be a good idea to make reservations for dinner together tonight."

"Jake, I can't think about dinner plans right now. I need to figure out how we're going to get through these negotiations tomorrow."

"Right." Jake straightened his posture. "What I meant was, since we lost a couple of days of work, I thought we could finalize the details of our plan tonight. I'm guessing we'll be working late."

"You're probably right," Emery sighed. "But I don't want it to be a big deal, or far away."

"How about the restaurant at the hotel?"

"Fine." Emery pursed her lips, the corners tilting up into a soft smile.

"See there? A healthy compromise." Jake beamed, lighting up the room as he sat back, proud of himself for breaking down Emery's hard shell once again.

A compromise … That was it! A light bulb went off in her head, and she picked up the phone and dialed Don Campbell's number.

"Don Campbell's office."

"Hi. It's Emery. Can I speak with Don, please?"

"I'll put you right through."

"Emerson, where the hell are you?"

"Don. I'm in the Medellín office. I have another way to get you your cost savings. We're canceling the negotiations tomorrow."

"What are you talking about? How?"

"You'll have our pitch next week."

"Monday morning, no later."

"Fine."

She hung up the phone. Jake's hands were gesticulating wildly in the air.

"What the heck was that? You have another solution?"

"Well no, not yet. But I just figured out that Don was open to a different solution, assuming I had one. I don't even know why I didn't think of compromising with Don before."

"You're crazy." Jake smiled. "We don't even have an idea!"

"Then we better get to work. Our pitch is Monday."

"Monday?" he gasped.

Emery picked up the phone again.

"Emerson Smith's office."

"Jeanine, I need you to cancel all appointments tomorrow. The negotiations are postponed until further notice. And please reschedule our flights. We'll leave tomorrow."

"Um, Ms. Smith. This is a lot to ask in such a short—"

"Yes, it is. And if you're not open to doing what I ask, coming to work on time, or letting me know about meetings in advance of their start times going forward, then you're fired. Do you understand me?"

"Yes, Ms. Smith."

Click.

Jake's mouth was agape. "Holy shit, Ms. Vice President. Where have you been?"

***

Emery walked out of the elevator to find Jake waiting for her in the lobby. His hands were in the pockets of his gray suit pants. He looked up and smiled.

Jake seemed relieved. "I was afraid you weren't going to show up."

"I'm here now. And we have work to do. Shall we?"

They walked into the hotel restaurant and were escorted to a dimly lit booth. They sat in rich burgundy leather seats. Tealight candles created a soft glow on Jake's face. He seemed worried, or cautious. Emery tried to read his expression.

The waiter approached. "May I start you off with a glass of wine?"

"I'll have the cabernet sauvignon," Emery said.

"Same," Jake said.

"At once," the waiter said, gliding down the aisle.

"Now about our pitch—"

"Emery, wait." Jake stopped her. "Is everything okay? You were really upset when I picked you up yesterday. Do you want to talk about it?" His hand inched toward her, but she pulled hers back.

Emery certainly did not want to talk about it. There was nothing to talk about anyway. She was moving on, and she needed to focus on her work and make things right for the Colombian farmers.

"Jake, I appreciate your concern. I'm fine now. I'd really like to discuss how we're going to solve this issue, though. We've been talking through ideas all day, but I don't feel like we're even close to a solution yet."

"Okay, okay." Jake's hands were up in surrender.

The hairs on the back of her neck stood on end and she turned to see a dark figure standing at the back of the restaurant. Emery squinted to get a sharper look, but the figure was gone. Emery shuddered.

"Did you see that?" she asked.

"I didn't." Jake stood to get a better look. He surveyed the restaurant until he seemed satisfied that there wasn't anything out of the ordinary. "There's no need to worry. You're with me."

"I guess I've been a little fidgety since that man attacked me the other night."

"If it makes you feel better, I can stay in your room tonight." He gave her a boyish grin.

She swatted his arm. "That obviously won't be necessary. And you need to stop flirting with me. I'm your boss. It's completely inappropriate."

"Whatever you say, boss." Unfazed, he casually took a sip of the wine that was set in front of him.

"Now about our pitch," Emery said, swirling her glass. She watched the tears of wine slowly drip down the edge, indicating it would be sweeter than a typical cabernet sauvignon. Her mouth watered in anticipation.

"Don is expecting us to come up with a cost savings pitch. But I might have a better idea," Emery said, taking a whiff of her wine. She smelled cranberries in a wooded forest grove. She savored the moment before taking her first sip, leaving Jake in suspense.

"Oh yeah? And what's that?"

"Something more long term. Sustainable," she said, looking up over her glass. "Organic."

"Organic coffee? What about the bugs? The infestation? Is this some mumbo jumbo that Luca fed to you while he had you trapped in his lair?"

Emery's heart quickened at the sound of Luca's name. Her cheeks flushed as a swirl of emotions, both lust and anger, surfaced on her skin. She picked up her wineglass coolly and took a deep breath.

"It's risky," Jake said.

"It is."

"You know we could lose our jobs over this, right?"

"I do," Emery said, taking her glass of wine and downing the rest of it in several large gulps.

Chapter 27

Luca blinked his eyes open. His mouth was dry, his teeth covered in a mossy film. His head pounded to the beat of his broken heart. He looked over at the empty bottle of rum sitting on the TV stand and let out a large sigh.

He had tried to drown out the vision of Fernando fluttering his eyes open for the last time. He needed to forget how Luisa fell to pieces in his arms, and that Juan and Mateo lost their big brother, without their father being there to comfort them. But the memories flooded back along with his consciousness.

He peeled himself off his couch and put his face in his hands. His reflection in the television set came back and slapped him across the face. His eyes were red and puffy. Luca reached for the carton of cigarettes sitting on his side table and lit one, letting the smoke coat his lungs and ease his aching nerves. He stared at the blazing cigarette and let it slowly burn.

He thought of Emery in his arms. The way she tasted in the rain. The fact that she looked just as beautiful in oversized overalls as she did in an elegant evening gown.

The cigarette burned toward his fingertips, and he pressed the butt into the ashtray.

Luca numbly walked over to the bathroom and turned on

the shower. He stood under the sputtering showerhead and hoped the lukewarm blanket would wash away the pain. But the water didn't clean anything. He still felt an empty pit of sadness as he got dressed and walked over to his brother's house to check on the twins.

A thick fog cloaked the plantation fields, with heavy rains in the distance. A strong wind urged him to quicken his pace down the gravel path. When he walked inside the house, Juan and Mateo were picking up broken glass from the ground. One of the chairs had been tipped over, and a football-sized dent in the wall appeared across the living room.

"What happened here?" Luca asked, stepping over the empty beer bottles thrown about the room. A dark mark stretched across the right side of Juan's jawline.

"What is this?" Luca asked, pulling Juan close to examine the mark.

"Dad came home last night. Drunk, of course. Tipping over furniture and throwing bottles," Juan said. "I accidentally got in the way."

Luca put his hands on Juan's shoulders to look him square in the eye. "Are you okay?"

"Sí," Juan said, puffing up his shoulders, trying to look strong.

"Where did your dad go?" Luca asked calmly.

"I'm not sure." Juan shrugged.

"He mentioned something about finding Emery Smith. He kept calling her names and stuff," Mateo said.

Luca's adrenaline spiked.

"Who is Emery Smith?" Juan asked.

"Do you know when he left?" Luca asked, his eyes darting toward the clock and back to Juan.

"A little while ago," Juan said.

"Are you boys going to be okay here? I'm going to go find him."

"We'll be fine," Mateo said.

Luca sprinted out of the house and ran to his truck, peeling out of the gravel road back to Medellín to catch Raphael before he could get to Emery again.

***

Jake watched Emery tilt her head back, letting the last drops of her fourth glass of wine fall onto her tongue. They had spent the past hour talking over the organic coffee pitch. Emery became more passionate about the topic as the night went on and the wine flowed.

She looked beautiful with her hair pulled back in a low bun. Her cheeks had become the cutest shade of pink, and her eyes glittered with determination in the flickering candlelight.

She was dead set on this organic pitch, but it was missing something. Don Campbell would need something more tangible than a marketing pitch. Jake's mind wandered while Emery talked on and on about the statistics of organic produce users.

Then, something Raphael had said popped in his mind. *"We're forced to buy cheap pesticides."* Why would he have used the word *forced*? Was that intentional?

Jake interrupted Emery's stream of consciousness. "Do you know anything about a company mandate that requires our growers to use a certain type of pesticide?" Jake asked.

Emery narrowed her focus on him. Deep in thought, she tilted her head to the side.

"I do recall one of the farmers saying something about

switching brands," she said. "Why do you ask?"

"I thought I heard someone say they were *forced* to use cheap pesticides."

"Do you think that was something Coffee Benz was behind?"

"Who else would it be?" Jake asked.

Emery traced her mouth with her fingernail while she thought it over. Her lips had turned a darker shade of pink from the wine. If they hadn't been having such a serious business conversation, he would have thought she was trying to seduce him.

"And why?" she asked. "Why would Coffee Benz care about what brand of pesticides they're using? For the control factor?"

"Or," Jake started. "They were benefiting from the mandate somehow."

"You're just speculating," Emery said, crossing her arms.

"I don't know. Maybe I am. But something is fishy."

"It's something worth looking into when we get back," Emery said, pinching the bridge of her nose. "Let's resume this conversation tomorrow. I'm tired, and we have an early flight."

"You got it, boss," Jake said, placing his napkin on the table.

Jake followed Emery out of the hotel restaurant. She walked a little wobbly on her two-inch black pumps and Jake put his arm around her shoulder to steady her.

"This is not me making a pass. This is me making sure we can walk in a straight line."

Emery murmured something under her breath, her eyelids getting heavier by the second.

They walked into an empty elevator and let the doors close them off from the humming hotel lobby. Emery let out a sigh of relief and reached around his torso, giving him an unexpected hug.

Jake was taken by surprise at first but then relished holding her. She was delicate and perfect under his arms. Her hair smelled like lavender and vanilla and looked so soft. It took every ounce of his willpower to not put his hands through it. She stayed in his arms the entire trip to her floor.

Was it the wine? Or was she starting to give in to her feelings for him? He didn't care what the reason was. He just wanted to hold her all night.

When the elevator doors opened, Emery let go and gave him an embarrassed smile.

"What was that for?" Jake smiled while holding the elevator door for her.

"I'm just really thankful you're in my life," she said, the right corner of her mouth curled in a half smile.

Jake's pulse quickened.

He walked her down the hotel hallway, fumbling with what to say and finding himself not knowing what to do with his hands. By the time they arrived at her hotel room, he awkwardly stood there hoping and wishing that she would let him in.

Emery unlocked the door and looked back at him. Her amber eyes were soft under heavy lids.

"Thank you. Thank you for being there for me," she said.

"You know I would do anything for you, Emery."

"See you bright and early for our flight," she said, slipping into her room.

"Yep," Jake said broken-heartedly. He took a step back, trying not to show the disappointment on his face.

The door shut, and Jake exhaled. He waited there for a moment, hoping that she would change her mind and let him in. After several painfully long seconds, he walked away and sulked back to his hotel room.

***

Emery flicked the fluorescent light of the bathroom. Her skin looked washed out against her wine-stained lips. She reached for the toothbrush and scrubbed away the stains on her teeth.

She couldn't tell if she'd had a fun evening with Jake, or if she was just riding the buzz of the fifth glass of wine.

Rinsing her face and patting it dry, she looked at her pale reflection in the mirror. Her hair was a little out of place, reminding her of Luca and his adorable morning bedhead, and the amazing dimpled smile that went—okay, what was she doing? Stop that! *He lied to you, remember?* The thought of Luca's betrayal spiraled her back into a state of despair.

She pouted her lower lip as she applied her ChapStick and came to terms with her current state of affairs. She would never see Luca again, and it was for her own good. As she sulked out of the bathroom, she flipped the hotel light on. A slight movement toward the back of the room caught her eye. A man was sitting in her hotel chair.

Emery's mouth fell open, too paralyzed to scream. She recognized him, the man from the gala. *Raphael.* She stumbled to get away, but his hands gripped her shoulders, pulling her away from the door and throwing her onto the bed.

He stalked toward her, his chest heaving. When the shadows shifted off his face, the light revealed glossy red eyes. Had he been crying?

Emery opened her mouth to scream, but he snorted and wiped away his tears with the back of his hand. He blubbered in Spanish, but Emery could not understand. He mumbled something about Fernando, triggering her memory, but she could not recall why. She watched him sink back into the chair and put his head in his hands. His shoulders were shaking with each sob.

She looked over at the phone next to her bed, and back at the crying intruder in her room. Slowly, she inched her hand toward the phone, but Raphael looked up before she could reach it. He torpedoed toward her and pulled the cord out of the jack, slamming the phone onto the floor.

Raphael's eyes blazed with fury, clear of sad tears and replaced with a dark hatred that made Emery tremble in fear.

"You killed my son," he said. He grabbed the standing lamp next to the bed and threw it down, shattering the bulb inside.

Emery winced at the impact, bracing herself for his next violent outburst.

"Raphael," Emery said through chattering teeth. "I am so sorry for your loss, but I did not kill your son."

He stood there silently for minutes before he broke down again, blubbering on about pesticides and coughing and a lot of incoherent Spanish that Emery could not understand. The rollercoaster ride of Raphael's emotions had Emery on edge. She looked for ways to escape the living nightmare but didn't want to snap Raphael out of his fragile state.

A knock on the door caused them both to jerk their heads up.

Raphael put his fingers to his lips, silencing Emery with a threatening glare. He quietly walked toward the door and peered through the peephole. He let out a heavy sigh as he rested his forehead on the door jam and clenched his fists.

"Emery?" Luca called from behind the door. "Emery, please, let me in. I think my brother is—"

Raphael opened the door. Luca stood in the hallway, his button-up shirt tucked in only halfway and his hair disheveled.

"Raphael? What have you done? Where's Emery?" Luca said, pushing past Raphael. He froze in his tracks. Emery was shaking on the bed.

"Are you okay?" Luca asked, pressing his gentle hands on her shoulders, scanning her body for any indication of harm.

"Your brother. He just showed up and started breaking things."

"Did he hurt you?"

Emery shook her head.

Luca let out a breath, and they both looked over at Raphael, who had shriveled up into a ball by the hotel door, incoherently muttering words and sobbing into his hands.

"I am so sorry. Raphael is not in his right mind, as you can see. I need to take him to the hospital."

"What's wrong with him?"

"He started losing his mind when his wife died a few years ago. But now," Luca choked on his words. "Now, he is grieving the loss of his son."

"Fernando?" Emery remembered where she had heard his name before. Luca's beloved nephew. "Luca, I don't know what to say. I am so sorry." Emery's hot tears burned down her cheeks.

"Fernando's death is no excuse for Raphael to show up and do this to you. I am so sorry for this. I will take care of him," Luca said.

Just then, Raphael got up and lunged onto Luca's back. Raphael's arms tightened around Luca's neck as he tried to wrestle him to the floor. Luca was able to break free and flipped Raphael onto the ground. Luca got on top of Raphael and growled in his face.

"Raphael! This ends now!"

Smack! Luca got a punch to the jaw that almost knocked him unconscious. Raphael struggled to get out from under Luca's weight, but Luca continued to pin him down.

"You're a traitor! You were going to sell us out! You're a backstabbing piece of shit!"

"Raphael, tranquilo," Luca said calmly. "Calm down, hermano. It's going to be okay." The soothing sound of Luca's voice eventually lulled Raphael back into his subdued state of despair. More tears ran down Raphael's cheeks as Luca cradled him in his arms.

"Come with me. It's going to be okay." Luca lifted his brother off the floor and wrapped his brother's limp arm around his neck to help him out of the hotel room. Before he left, he looked over his shoulder at Emery. "We will finish this conversation when I get back."

Once the door closed, Emery broke down on the hotel bed, sobbing into her pillow. The terror of finding Raphael in her room was enough to bring her to tears, but she found herself mourning for Luca instead.

Emery's chest felt heavy with doubt. She struggled to hold on to the anger she felt for Luca. It didn't feel plausible that Luca could have planned Raphael's episode at the gala just to get her out to the farm. Raphael was actually sick.

Plus, the negotiations had been canceled. If their stunt at the gala had been one big plan to stop the negotiations, then why pull another ruse now?

A soft knock came from door. Her heart leapt into her throat, and she ran to open it.

Jake stood casually in his unbuttoned shirt. His hair was

newly washed and tousled to one side. Emery was so disappointed it wasn't Luca that she fell to her knees and continued to cry in her hands.

"Emery, what's wrong?" Jake knelt down and put his arms around her, stroking her back as she buried her head into his chest.

"Shh. It's okay. I know this has been really hard."

Emery's sobs started to subside, and she wondered about Jake's meaning.

"I know that our working environment requires a platonic relationship, but we can work something out, right? I mean, I can find a different position at Coffee Benz, and we can be together, forever. Emery, I've always loved you, and only you."

Emery froze in complete shock, her chin nearly hitting the floor. She couldn't believe what she was hearing. The next thing she knew, Jake cupped Emery's stunned face and planted a kiss on her open mouth. It took a blink for Emery to push him away in horror. Behind Jake, she saw Luca standing down the hall in a hot rage.

"Luca!" she cried out, but he turned around and headed back to the elevators.

Emery released herself from Jake's grasp and ran down the hall in time to watch Luca get in the elevator.

"Stop, please," she gasped, trying to catch her breath. She stood in front of the elevator as the doors began to close. Luca's jaw clenched tight, and he stared blankly as if his eyes had turned to stone.

"Luca," she pleaded.

He said nothing, letting the elevator doors close between them.

Chapter 28

The elevator made the slow descent downward, a journey that felt infinitely longer than it should have. The farther Luca got from Emery, the more his blood boiled with fury. His chest ached at the image of Emery in Jake's arms. His mouth on her lips. He could have killed Jake right then and there, but how could he? What if she loved *him* instead?

The elevator walls inched closer, confining him like a caged animal. He couldn't breathe. He had to get out.

At the sixth floor, the elevator stopped. A young couple stepped on, hand in hand, dressed for a fancy evening out. The man's cologne smacked Luca in the face, and the doors closed behind them, giving Luca very little room to breathe. He was trapped more than ever. They giggled in the corner of the elevator, the sound of happiness like shrapnel to Luca's heart.

They finally reached the first floor. When the doors opened to the main lobby, Luca stepped out, sucking in a deep, long breath.

"Señor Mendoza. Is now a good time?"

Luca looked at the officer with a thick, white mustache and heavy creases around his mouth. He was carrying a small notepad in his hand and a radio phone in the other.

"Can we talk outside? I need a smoke."

The officer nodded and followed him out the main lobby doors. The cool night air helped wick away the beaded sweat that had accumulated on Luca's forehead. He pulled out a cigarette and took a long drag before telling the officer everything.

"So he's been acting erratically for a couple of years now?" the officer asked, jotting in his notepad.

Luca nodded, blowing out the puff of smoke he was holding in his lungs.

"He doesn't belong in jail. He just needs a doctor."

"Well, it all depends on whether Ms. Smith wants to press charges or not."

Luca clenched his jaw. He pressed the cigarette butt under his heel and kicked a small rock with the point of his shoe.

An officer appeared through the main lobby doors, holding Raphael by the handcuffs behind his back. Raphael lumbered forward, looking up at Luca just before the officer placed a hand on his head, guiding him into the police car. Raphael's betrayed look crushed what was left of Luca's heart.

"How could you do this to me?" Raphael shouted through the police car window.

The words pounded around in his chest and between his temples. As the police car drove out of the porte cochere, Luca ran his hands through his hair, regretting everything. He had turned his own brother in to the cops. For what? For Emery? What good was that now?

He kicked another rock but felt no relief. He wished he had never taken Emery back to the plantation. He had known she belonged to Jake from the moment they met. She was just too blind to see it for herself.

***

Emery opened the door to her condo and released the heavy luggage onto the tile floor. The lids of her eyes felt heavy and weak as she switched the kitchen light on. She looked around to find everything in its right place. Clean, perfect, and sterile. She examined her blank, taupe walls and pristine white furniture. It felt like something was missing. Her condo had been orchestrated with such meticulous precision, there was no room for any actual life there.

She plopped herself on her kitchen barstool, her head in her hands. She had spent the entire trip from Colombia fretting over Luca. There was still so much more to be said. She wasn't sure she could trust him. He proved to her he did not scheme with his brother by turning him in to the police. She didn't have the heart to press charges under the condition he received psychiatric help. But there was still the matter of the other woman. Emery would never forget the image of Esmeralda lunging at her in front of the stables. She shuddered at the thought of Luca with a woman like that.

Emery's stomach growled for attention. She hadn't eaten anything but a bag of peanuts on the plane. Her refrigerator had a jar of pickles and a small wedge of cheese. She huffed and slammed the door closed. Perhaps crawling into bed was her only option.

As she walked out of the kitchen, the red flashing light on her answering machine caught her eye.

"You have two new messages. First message: Hi, sweetie. It's your dad. Mom and I are taking a last-minute trip to Tampa, Florida. We'll call you from our hotel in a couple of days. What's that? Oh okay. Mom says hi. All right, Emy. Talk soon.

Love you.

"Next message: Emerson. This is Don. I just got off the phone with Jake, and I want to make it clear how serious our situation is. Your job is on the line. Monday's proposal better be good. Also, I have a meeting with our CBP division that morning, so we have to cut your proposal short to thirty minutes. See you Monday."

The weight of stress crushed her already-tired spirit. Emery reached for the cordless phone and thumped on the dial pad.

"Hello?"

"Jake. It's me."

"Hey there, Ems. What can I do for ya?"

"Did Don call you, or did you call him?" Emery asked.

"He called me, why? Didn't he call you too?"

"Yeah, I just don't understand why you're the *first one* he calls. Why would he have hired me as the VP if he's just going to—"

Emery stopped her train of thought as her mind stuck on something in Don's voice mail that didn't sound familiar.

"Ems? You there?" Jake asked.

"What is the CBP division?" Emery asked.

"I have no idea. Never heard of it."

"Well, apparently we will only have thirty minutes to run our pitch because Don is meeting with the CBP division, whatever that means. I know we discussed some of our ideas earlier, but we'll really need to hammer this proposal out over the weekend. Do you mind coming into the office tomorrow?"

"Spend the weekend with you? I don't mind at all." Emery could hear his smile over the phone.

"Don't get any ideas. As we discussed after last night's incident, we're just friends," Emery scolded.

"I know. I know. Okay, I'll see you in the office tomorrow."

"Thank you. Good night, Jake."

"Good night, boss."

***

Jake's footsteps echoed down the hall as he made his way to Emery's office. He slowed his pace. He wasn't alone. Emery's office lamp was on. Through the glass window, Emery's head rested in her hands. Her shoulders were shaking. Soft sniffles made their way through the windowpane.

Jake lightly knocked on the door, hoping he wouldn't scare her. Emery's head jerked up. She grabbed a tissue from her desk to dry her eyes.

"Hey. You okay?"

"Ugh. I'm so embarrassed. I'm a mess. I'm sorry."

"Ems, you don't need to apologize. I'm embarrassed. I'm sorry about what happened too."

"No, it's not that." Emery paused.

"Is it Luca?" Jake hated himself for asking. He already knew the answer.

Emery blew her nose. She tried to compose herself and threw the tissue in the wastebasket. She had given herself to Luca, and all that was left of them was in the garbage.

"It doesn't matter. He has a *girlfriend.* He lied to me. So, that's that," Emery said. Jake fidgeted with his fingers while she gathered the stack of papers on her desk and placed her calculator on top. "I have a few things I want to show you for our pitch. Shall we work in the conference room?"

Emery tried putting a smile on her face, but Jake could see through it. She started to march out of her office, but Jake stopped her, placing a hand on her shoulder.

"I'm so sorry about that kiss. I didn't realize you and Luca were—"

"Luca and I are nothing. Let's just forget it, okay?" she said, brushing past him.

"Whatever you say, boss," Jake said. "I'll meet you in the room. I just have to take care of something first."

Jake stepped into his office and gently shut the door. He couldn't believe what he was about to do. But he couldn't stand seeing Emery so miserable. He logged onto his computer and opened up their database.

He stared at the phone as if it were personally assaulting him, and hesitated for several moments before he could muster the courage to dial the number. Seven painfully long rings later, someone finally picked up.

"Hola?" said the voice on the other end.

"Hi. Is Luca Mendoza available?" he said, closing his eyes with instant regret.

"This is Luca. Who is this?"

"It's Jake."

There was a long pause.

"You son of a bitch! Why are you calling me? To gloat? Is that it?"

"Luca, I can explain. Emery had nothing to do with that kiss."

"Give me a break," Luca scoffed.

"Dude, you have to understand me. That was my fault. I saw her crying, and I completely misread her. She doesn't want me. She made it very clear. The thing is," Jake faltered, not sure if he should continue. "She is in love with *you*," he said, pounding the phone on his forehead. The jab to his skull was nothing compared to the jab to his pride, and yet he continued.

"Qué?" Luca asked. "Are you telling me there isn't something going on between you two?"

"That's exactly what I'm telling you, man. I am really sorry if I got in the way. Emery never gave me the time of day, all right? And it pains me to say all that because I hate you and all, but she is a mess without you."

Silence.

"Why are you telling me this?" Luca asked.

"Because I'm a nice guy," Jake said.

Luca was quiet.

"And because I need your help."

"There it is."

"Emery and I are going to present to the CEO of our company on Monday. I think she's going to lose her job because we didn't follow through with the negotiations. Plus, she has this whole pitch idea about organic coffee. Don is not going to go for it. I already know it. He told me over the phone last night that I am next in line after this whole presentation blows up in her face."

"What's wrong with her idea?"

"I just know it's not going to work. Don is old school. He's not going to buy into her crazy ideas about cutting out the pesticides. I need you to talk to her."

"Cutting out the pesticides is actually a really good idea. We would cut our costs, and …" The phone went silent.

"Hello?" Jake said. "You still there?"

"Oh my God. Why didn't I think of this before? The *pesticides* are what's killing the people down here."

"What? How do you mean?"

"There's been four cases of people, including my nephew, dying of some kind of lung condition. They all worked on coffee farms. It's got to be that."

"But that doesn't make sense. You guys have been using the same pesticides for years. Why would it cause problems now?"

"Actually we just switched brands. And it wasn't that long ago."

"Switched to what?"

"I don't remember. Raphael was handling it," Luca said. "It was something called CBD or CBP. I can't recall."

"Hold on a second," Jake said. "Did you just say CBP?"

"Yeah, I think that's right."

"I've got an idea. How fast can you get a plane to Chicago?"

***

Emery was looking over her paperwork when Jake walked into the conference room.

"Where have you been?" Emery asked, tapping her pen on the desk.

"Making you coffee," Jake said, smiling behind a steaming cup.

He was lying, but she was grateful anyway. She had forgotten to pour herself coffee earlier that morning, and her head was aching from withdrawal.

"Thank you." She smiled into her coffee, taking her first sip. She felt the color return to her cheeks.

"You're welcome," Jake said, taking a seat next to Emery. He brought his own stack of papers and made a couple of piles across the table.

"Ems, before we get started. I have to tell you something about that lady who screamed at you in front of the farm."

Emery rolled her eyes. "Ugh, Jake, I don't—"

"Listen. Um, she is *not* Luca's girlfriend."

"What?"

"Esmeralda thinks she's his girlfriend, but she's really just a filthy whore. She has been in love with Luca for a long time. She's completely looney tunes for him. From what I heard, he never calls her, he doesn't like her, but she continues to throw herself at him."

"So." Emery was trying to piece this together. "Then how did you and Esmeralda—"

"Never mind that. It's a long story." Jake scratched his head. "I thought it would be better if you knew the truth about Luca."

"And what's the truth?"

"The truth is," Jake cringed. "He's not a bad guy. In fact, I think he actually might be in love with you."

"How would you know?"

"Because I know. I saw the look on his face. I wanted to punch his teeth in, but I could tell he cared about you."

Emery's heart fluttered. She wanted to believe Jake. But she still wasn't sure she could trust him. She didn't know what to think. Her head was spinning.

"Ems, there's one other thing."

"What is it?"

"It's about CBP."

***

Emery and Jake worked on their presentation all day. They were putting the final touches on the financials board when Emery decided they were done. The sun was low on the horizon, pounding through the conference room window.

Emery took a step back and looked at their poster boards.

Jake stood next to her with his hands on his hips.

"I think we've got it," Emery said confidently.

"I do too," Jake said, patting Emery on the shoulder.

"What if Don questions the link between the CBP division and the pesticide-related deaths? What if he doesn't believe us?"

"Let me take care of that."

Emery gave a sigh of relief. "Great. Okay, I'm going to run through this on my own. I'll let you know if I think we need to meet up tomorrow."

"I'm going to head out then," Jake said as he gathered his things to leave.

"Thank you, Jake. You've been a huge help," Emery said, smiling at him as he left the room.

Jake gave her a salute and walked out the door.

Emery stared at her presentation, but her mind pulled her back to the unfinished business with Luca. She tapped her pencil nervously as she thought about what to do. She needed to talk to him. Set things straight. She needed answers.

Emery sat down at her computer and opened the database with all the farmers' contact information. She searched for Mendoza and stared at his phone number on the screen. A chunk of something crumbled in her mouth and she realized she had chewed the end of her pencil eraser. Emery spat it out.

Picking up the phone, she slowly dialed the number on the screen. Her heart pounded. Her breathing picked up. She fidgeted with the loose strand of hair that fell in front of her eyes while the phone rang.

"Hola?" said a young voice on the other line.

"Hi, may I speak with Luca Mendoza, please?"

"He's not here. Can I take a message?"

"Um, sure. I'm …" Emery hesitated. "Actually, can I try back tomorrow?"

"He's gone for a few days, but he should be back by Wednesday, I think."

Emery counted the days in her head. Three more days until she could speak to him again. She wasn't sure she could wait that long, but she wasn't given a choice.

"Oh, okay. I'll try again later," Emery said. She let out the air she had been holding in and anxiously tapped her pencil until it snapped in half, sending the chewed-eraser end across the room.

Chapter 29

Luca got out of the cab and scanned the high-rise building until he saw the blue morning sky. He reached for his pack of cigarettes that were tucked away in his suit jacket pocket. Nervously, he held the lighter in front of the cigarette and flicked on the flame. A mass of people stampeded along the sidewalks. Many of them were sipping on their to-go coffee cups with plastic lids. They all rushed past each other, in a hurry to get to their desk jobs. Luca contemplated Emery's life here while he puffed on his cigarette.

The honking of the taxi drivers grew louder as more and more people flooded the streets of Chicago. People crowded the sidewalk, and Luca couldn't seem to find a place to stand and smoke without being in the way.

"Luca!" yelled a familiar voice.

Luca turned around. Jake was walking out of the building turnstiles. The smug bastard was dressed like a catalog model. He wore a sleek gray suit and shiny deep mahogany oxfords.

Luca looked down at his plain brown business suit and plaid button-up shirt and shrugged.

Jake walked up and held out his hand. Luca threw down his cigarette and stomped on it before grabbing Jake's firm grip.

"Buenos días."

"Ditto," Jake said, looking up at the bright sky. His hands perched on his hips. The stream of people parted around them.

"How was the flight?" Jake asked.

"Good, thank you," Luca said, his nerves creeping back up again. "How's Emery?"

"She's good. Nervous for the pitch, but we've got a solid proposal," Jake said. "It'll be good to have you here for backup." He slapped Luca on the back. "Now let's get you inside."

"What did Emery say when you told her I was coming?"

"Oh. I, uh, actually … I haven't mentioned it yet."

"Qué?" He grabbed Jake's shoulders and looked him straight in the eye.

"She doesn't know I'm here? What were you thinking?" Luca's grip tightened.

"Well, I wasn't sure if you were going to make it. I didn't want to get her hopes up."

Luca ignored Jake's insult, and he gripped Jake's shoulders harder.

"Calm down, man. It's going to be fine. We'll go up there right now and get everything squared away before our meeting."

"Isn't the meeting in ten minutes?" Luca asked, more aggressively than he meant to.

"Yep. We better hurry."

Jake appeared to be relishing in the fact that Luca was obviously agitated and nervous to see Emery.

"Lead the way then," Luca said flatly.

"Please. After you," Jake said, ceremoniously holding his hand out toward the turnstile doors, clearly wasting more time than was necessary.

"Por favor. After you." Luca stepped back, letting Jake go ahead.

Their elevator ride was thick with tension. Luca cursed himself for having trusted Jake with the plan. Jake casually put his hands in his pockets, rocking back and forth on his heels, whistling a tune that Luca recognized but couldn't place.

When the elevator doors opened, Jake politely held the doors for Luca to get out first. Luca sneered and stepped out. He hated that his heart was beating so hard that he could feel the pulse in his ears. The skin around his neck felt warm and itchy from the cheap wool fabric of his dated business suit.

They walked down a long hallway toward a woman with wild fire-red hair sitting at a desk. She was chewing gum and typing on the computer in front of her when they walked up.

"Jeanine. I'd like to introduce you to Luca Mendoza," Jake said.

Jeanine's mouth dropped, letting the gum fall out and onto her keyboard. She sat frozen for a moment before she snapped out of her trance. She gave a flirty smile and batted her eyelashes as she tried to discreetly pick up her chewing gum from her keyboard and throw it in the trash.

"Good morning, Mr. Mendoza. How can I help you?" She twirled one of her loose red curls around her finger.

"Where's Emery?" Jake asked.

Without releasing her focus on Luca, Jeanine said, "I believe she's in the conference room getting set up. Can I get you anything, honey? A cup of coffee? Water? Tea?"

"No, thank you," Luca said, looking around nervously.

"Oh my. I can tell from your accent that you're not from around here. Colombia, I assume?" she swooned.

"Sí." Luca shifted his attention to Jake. "Shall we head to the conference room?"

Jake led Luca to a conference room. Poster boards with graphs and numbers were displayed around a long rectangular table with black leather seats.

He looked at the wall clock. They only had five more minutes until their meeting was supposed to start.

"Why don't you take a seat? I'm sure she'll be right back."

"This is cutting it a little close, don't you think?" Luca asked as he walked around the table and gripped one of the leather chairs. He was filled with so much angst, he thought he might tear through the leather with his bare hands.

"Nervous, buddy?" Jake gloated.

"No, but, it's not really how I envisioned—"

Just then a stern older gentleman with a briefcase walked in. He stopped when he saw Luca standing behind one of the chairs.

"Don!" Jake said in a booming voice. "Good morning, sir. This is Luca Mendoza. He'll be joining us this morning to talk more about what's going on in Colombia."

Don reached out to Luca. "Mr. Mendoza. Welcome."

***

Emery had just finished putting up her boards and stepped back with her hands on her hips. She was proud of the work she and Jake had put together, but her nerves were taking over. Her hand trembled slightly as she picked up the printed copies of her brief and placed them at the head of the table.

This presentation was more than just her normal business proposal pitch. Her job was at stake. More importantly, there were actual lives at stake.

She looked at the wall clock. She still had six minutes until Don was going to show up for the presentation. She was starting to feel suffocated by the conference room. She needed a moment to breathe and get away from her boards and graphs. She decided to grab some coffee from the breakroom.

Her high heels clicked on the floor as she made her way to the room across the hall. She grabbed a mug from the cupboard. As she poured her coffee, she heard a muffled sound of men talking. It almost sounded like she might have heard Luca's voice.

I must be going crazy, she thought.

She took a sip of coffee and let the steam fill her nose. She already felt rejuvenated. As she walked back to the boardroom, she stopped short. She had to blink a few times before realizing she was looking at Don shaking hands with *Luca*. Luca!

What the hell is going on?

She looked over to Jake, who stood at the back of the room. He gave her an apologetic look and mouthed the words *I'm sorry*.

Emery looked back at Luca, and their eyes locked on to each other. His freshly shaved skin, piercing blue eyes, and dreamy dimples took her breath away. Her legs felt weak, and the sound of her thumping heart in her ears prevented her from hearing his words.

"Luca," Emery stammered. "I'm sorry I wasn't expecting you to be here." She looked over her shoulder at Jake for an answer.

"Luca is here to help us with the last part of our pitch."

Emery swallowed her anxiety and gave Luca a polite smile.

"It's a pleasure to see you, Luca. Please sit." She turned to Don for a distraction. "Good morning, Don. You ready to begin?" Emery asked, trying to keep her voice from quivering.

"Let's hear it, Emerson."

Don was in a bad mood. Emery could feel it.

Jake and Luca took a seat across from each other as Don sat at the head of the table. Emery still couldn't believe Luca was in the conference room. This is the last place she had expected to see him again. Luca looked up at her with an encouraging smile, which flustered her even more.

Emery cleared her throat as she pulled her presentation boards forward. The skin around her neck turned red as her anxious nerves got the best of her. She gave Jake one more reprimanding glance before she began.

"Don, I fully recognize the severity of our situation, and why I was asked to start up the negotiations in Medellín. There were some unexpected events that occurred while I was there that opened my eyes." Emery paused to look at Luca, who was leaning forward, listening intently.

"It's all in the numbers. Jake's going to take you through some facts before I propose a solution to pull this company out of its rut."

Jake got up and stood next to one of the easels at the head of the table. "Thanks for the setup, Emery." He flashed his award-winning grin. His confidence immediately filled the room, and Don visibly relaxed in his chair.

"A couple of years ago, we went through the last round of negotiations, cutting our costs by five percent. The farmers were ticked off, to say the least."

Luca choked on his water. "Pardon," he said.

"Get to the point, Whitmore," Don said, leaning back in his chair.

"At the same time we cut the prices, our company sent out a corporate mandate to all our associated coffee farmers that stated everyone needs to get on the pesticide bandwagon to ensure an increase in our supply. What you'll see in this chart is that even though our inventory increased, our quality ratings and wholesale volumes have been on the steady decline.

"If we were to cut costs again, it would only perpetuate the problem, as many coffee growers would go out of business. Not only would we get a decrease in supply, but the quality and sales volumes would continue to decline, not helping the profitability problem we're having now."

"Is that right, Mendoza? Would an easy five percent reduction in costs really put farmers out of business?" Don asked.

Luca looked squarely in Don's eyes and nodded. "Any reduction in costs would put me out of the coffee business entirely. We're stripped down to bare bones."

Emery stood and walked over to another poster board with more graphs.

"Don, we looked at several years of history and found that when our pricing is stabilized around six to seven percent above the market average, the quality rates range ten to fifteen percent higher than the market average. When this happens, our wholesale volume is at its highest. Plus, history tells us that we peaked in revenue before pesticides were being used as much as they are now."

"Emery, are you suggesting we cut pesticides? That is not happening," Don interjected.

"Hear me out, Don." Emery paused. "It is a common misperception that if we don't use pesticides, it will affect the supply in a negative way, but there is no evidence that is the case. In fact, there is evidence that if you go organic, and you market yourself as organic, the consumer sales lift can reach as high as three hundred percent."

"What do you mean, 'go organic'?" Don asked, pulling his glasses off his nose.

"There is an organic movement happening in the industry right now, and research shows that consumers care about organic products. Consumers are willing to pay up to two times more for a cup of organic coffee over non-organic."

Emery pointed to her chart and got a glimpse of Luca's starstruck face. She blushed before continuing.

"If you want to fix the margin issue in this company, then we need to fix our quality first. And we can fix our quality by paying our farmers six percent above the market average, cutting out the pesticides and marketing ourselves as an organic coffee distributor."

"Do you know how much money that would cost to 'go organic,' as you say? We're talking a lot of money, sweetheart," Don scoffed.

Emery flinched at the patronizing tone, but she stood her ground.

"It would require a little bit of an investment up front, but with a modest eight percent increase in retail sales prices, and a conservative ten percent lift in our wholesale volume, our margin rate will turn around in less than one year. I estimate that our profits would increase by twenty-eight percent in two years."

Emery paused to let that sink in.

"And, we could get that double-digit margin increase in two years while paying the farmers about two percent more than what they are getting now."

"Emerson, this sounds like a long-term solution. What are we going to do about the last two quarters of the year? What's stopping me from cutting out production in Colombia, and expanding our farmers' base in Ethiopia?"

Emery froze. She had forgotten about Ethiopia. She didn't know enough about it to respond. Her mouth went dry, as she struggled to form words.

"Ethiopia?" she stalled. "I ... uh ... don't think it—"

"I wouldn't do that if I were you," Luca chimed in.

Emery turned to look at Luca, her eyes wide.

"Oh yeah? And why is that?" Don crossed his arms.

Luca cleared his throat. "First of all, if you took your business out of Colombia, don't you think that would make the news? Leaving thousands of coffee farmers without paying jobs? And if you don't think that would be bad enough publicity, then you need to consider the type of publicity you would get when the press finds out about the increasing number of deaths among Coffee Benz farmers."

Don shifted in his chair. "What do you mean, deaths?"

"Deaths due to pesticide use. Cheap pesticide use. The cheapest kind on the market, in fact."

Don's nostrils flared, but Luca pressed on.

"A few of the deaths that I know, including my teenage nephew," Luca continued. "And they had something in common. You think you might know what that might be?"

Don gave Luca an icy glare. He said nothing, which seemed to fuel Luca's confidence.

"What they had in common was that they were using the same brand of pesticides: CBP," Luca said. "Perhaps you've heard of it?"

"Are you threatening me, Mendoza?" Don stood and looked around the room. He was cornered and red-faced. Emery's heart beat so hard in her chest, she was sure Luca heard it too. They exchanged concerned glances while Don gathered his things.

"So what do you want from me?" Don asked.

"Listen to Emery. It sounds like she has a pretty good plan to get you out of this mess," Luca said smugly. "That, and you'll have to shut down your CBP division."

Don collected his day planner and started walking out of the room. Before stepping through the door, he turned to look back at Emery.

"Emerson. I will speak with you later."

Emery blinked, and Don was gone.

***

Luca's blood pressure was at an all-time high. He needed a cigarette. He watched Emery, standing in Don's wake, processing what had just transpired in the boardroom. Her amber eyes made their way back to Luca, and they softened as the air released from her lungs. Her hair was pulled back, and she was wearing a little makeup on her face, covering the adorable freckles he missed so much.

"Welp," Jake broke the silence. "That was about as good as it could have gone, I think."

"Why didn't you tell me you were coming?" Emery asked.

"Uh, well, I wanted to—"

"That was my fault," Jake interrupted. "I was going to tell you. I guess I wasn't sure if it was going to work out."

"So you orchestrated this whole thing?" Emery asked Jake.

"Yeah. I did." Jake popped out of his chair. "Now, I'm guessing you two have some catching up to do." He started walking out the door when Jeanine popped her head into the conference room. She fixated on Luca, undressing him with her eyes. "Ms. Smith. Your next meeting starts in five minutes."

"Shoot." Emery looked around the room and back at Luca.

"Go ahead. Come find me later. I'll clean up the room and wait in your office until you get back."

"You sure?" Emery asked.

"Of course."

"I can keep him company, Ms. Smith. Don't you worry about a thing," Jeanine said slyly.

Emery pouted. "Thank you, Luca," she said apologetically and left the conference room.

Jeanine watched him as if he were a piece of meat. Luca nervously took down the posters and easels and gathered the printed documents as Jeanine continued to stare at him from across the room.

"So, Luca. Will you be staying in Chicago long?" Jeanine asked.

"I leave tomorrow," Luca said curtly, carrying as many posters as he could.

"So soon? That's a shame. I would love to take you around Chicago," she said, following him out.

Luca stopped midstep. He didn't know how to get to Emery's office. He looked at Jeanine, hoping that she would lead the way. Instead, Jeanine buckled at the knees.

"My goodness, you have the most stunning blue eyes I have ever seen."

"Could you point me to Emery's office, por favor?" Luca asked.

"Oh, of course," she said, a little rejected.

Jeanine was sure to pat him on the shoulder as she opened Emery's office door. She kept her hand there for an uncomfortably long time before turning away.

Luca closed the door, relieved to be away from Jeanine. He could still feel her eyes on the back of his neck through the glass wall. When he looked over his shoulder, Jeanine was biting her knuckle. She quickly jerked around and attended to her computer's keyboard.

Luca pulled the blinds down, shutting off the fishbowl effect of Emery's office. He looked around. No personal objects of any kind. No pictures on the walls. A cardboard box was pushed against the wall with stacks of folders and binders.

He thought back to the presentation. Emery was incredible in there. It was clear that she was made for this business stuff. It was as if she was born for it.

Luca played with her pen holder and examined each utensil. Among the blue and black pens, he found a pencil with a chunk bitten off of the eraser.

A knock on the door interrupted his thoughts, and Jake popped his head in. His slicked hair had started to come undone, and a tousled chunk fell over his forehead.

"Hey, buddy, can I get you anything? Coffee? Tea?"

"No, thank you."

"Okay, man. I just wanted to say that you did a good job in there. I'm glad you came," Jake said.

Luca looked at him inquisitively but decided to take the compliment.

"Gracias."

"So, you and Emery …" Jake started.

"I don't know. I guess I'll just have to wait and see."

Jake nodded, his hands on his hips as he bit his lower lip. Deep in thought for a moment, he finally looked up to say, "Whatever happens, just know that if you hurt her, I'm going to mess you up."

Luca's eyebrows rose at Jake's threat. "Understood."

***

Emery rushed out of her meeting, anxious to see Luca. She stepped in the ladies' restroom to look herself over. She examined her white button-up blouse for any creases and smoothed out her navy-blue pencil skirt. Satisfied, she placed a thin layer of lip balm over her lips and patted her cheeks to bring out her natural rosy color. She wasn't sure what she was going to say to Luca at first, but she couldn't wait to get her arms around him and apologize for leaving him in Colombia without saying goodbye.

She charged out of the bathroom. As she turned the corner, a tall man suddenly appeared, and they crashed into each other. The jostled man had been walking with a mug of coffee, which spilled down Emery's white blouse. Coffee dripped from her nose as she stood in the hallway in complete horror.

"Oh my goodness. I am so sorry," the man said, brushing off the coffee that landed on his tie.

"It's okay. It's okay." Emery looked down. Her blouse looked like a Pollock painting. She froze in the hallway, not knowing if she should try to salvage her shirt or just keep walking toward her office.

"Can I get you some paper towels or something?"

"No, no. It's okay. I'll be fine." Emery stood up straight.

She walked steadily down the long hallway to her office. Jeanine looked up from her computer, and her mouth gaped open. Emery ignored Jeanine's gaze and opened her office door to find Luca sitting in the chair across from her desk. When she walked in, his eyes grew round like giant blue saucers.

"What happened to you?" He stood, placing an object he had been fidgeting with in his pant pocket. "Are you okay?"

"I'm fine," Emery said, looking at herself in the small compact mirror she had in her desk drawer. "But seriously, how does this keep happening?"

Luca tilted his head back for a hearty laugh and grabbed a tissue from her desk. He walked over to Emery and pressed the tissue where coffee had splattered on her upper lip. His touch sent a jolt of sensation down Emery's spine.

"Do you have something under your blouse?" Luca asked.

"A camisole, yes." Emery looked up into Luca's piercing eyes.

"Unbutton your shirt," Luca directed.

Emery nearly melted into a puddle and obediently unbuttoned her shirt, revealing her satin camisole with lace straps underneath.

Luca took her stained shirt from her hands and walked out of the office. He closed the door, leaving Emery breathless. A moment later, he returned without the shirt and gave her a mischievous smile.

"What did you do with my shirt?"

"I gave it to your administrative assistant to rinse and dry for you."

"Oh." Emery was surprised that Jeanine would even do something like that for her. "Thanks. About the other night," Emery started.

"Jake told me everything," Luca stopped her, placing a finger on her lips. "He also told me what happened when Esmeralda showed up—"

"I know," Emery interrupted, mimicking Luca as she put her finger up to his lips.

They stood there, silencing each other. Without saying a word, Emery and Luca came to a silent understanding. For the first time since the moment they met, Emery could breathe peacefully. She studied his expression as his eyes gravitated to her shoulder.

The lace strap of her camisole slipped off her shoulder, sending shivers down her skin. Luca's fingers came in to rescue it. He slipped his forefinger under the delicate fabric and caressed her arm as he put the strap in place.

Luca's touch triggered something in Emery that she couldn't contain anymore. As she reached for Luca's mouth, he crashed into hers. Luca's hands traveled from her knees to her hips as he reacquainted himself with her body. He lifted her legs until she straddled him on her office desk.

Emery's camisole had shifted past her breasts, exposing her to Luca's mouth as he took in her nipple and swirled his tongue around. Emery let out a soft whimper as her body contracted against his mouth.

Luca tugged on Emery's hair, releasing her bun. He wrapped his hand around the auburn strands to guide her head back, giving him easy access to her neck. Emery purred under his hot, wet tongue.

Luca pressed himself against her panties, and a fiery heat kindled between her legs. Emery grabbed at his broad, muscular back, pulling him closer, about to lose herself to him when a knock came from the door.

Knock, knock.

Luca leaped into the chair across the room as Emery frantically smoothed out her skirt. She was pulling her hair back into a ponytail when Jeanine's head poked around the door.

"Yes?" Emery asked coolly.

"Your shirt should be dry momentarily. I just wanted to let you know that I rescheduled your appointments this afternoon in case you wanted to go home and change." Jeanine raised an eyebrow toward Luca, who was trying to look casual in the office chair.

"Thank you, Jeanine. I'll send Luca to retrieve my shirt in a few minutes."

Jeanine nodded and closed the door behind her.

Emery let out the air she had been holding in.

"That was close," Emery said.

Chapter 30

Luca and Emery walked down the block to a small Italian pizzeria with red-and-white-checkered plastic tablecloths. The restaurant was full of people talking loudly over the accordion music in the background.

Emery spotted a booth toward the back of the restaurant and took Luca's hand to lead him to the table. As they passed the kitchen counter, a heavyset Italian man with a thick black mustache looked up and beamed at her.

"Emersonia!" he said.

Emery smiled and waved. "Hi, Antonio."

Luca's eyes shifted between Emery and Antonio.

"First Jake. Now Antonio? Who else do I have to be jealous of?" Luca said teasingly.

Emery laughed at his joke. She tossed her ponytail over her shoulder as she took a seat.

"This is my favorite place in Chicago. My dad and I used to come here when I was a kid. Antonio is like an uncle to me."

Luca watched Emery as she smiled at Antonio, who had walked over toward their booth. Luca was mesmerized by how she could look so mature one minute, and so youthful in another.

Antonio reached down to give Emery a kiss on the cheek.

He whispered in her ear, although not soft enough, as Luca heard him ask, "Who is the guy?"

"Antonio, I'd like you to meet Luca. He's from Colombia," she said with a sparkle in her eye.

"Welcome to the best pizzeria in Chicago. You are one lucky man to be here with Emersonia. She usually eats alone."

"Lucky indeed."

"What'll it be today? The usual?"

"Pepperoni and mushrooms okay with you?" Emery asked.

"Bueno," Luca said.

"Coming right up," Antonio said, walking over to the bar and bringing back two glasses of red wine.

"Antonio, I didn't—"

"It's on the house. Enjoy." Antonio gave her a pat on the shoulder. As he walked away, he started talking with the couple sitting in the booth behind them, gesticulating wildly, while the couple laughed at his joke.

"He seems nice," Luca said, grabbing his glass of wine. He raised it to her, and she followed.

"To an incredible presentation given by the most amazing woman I have ever known."

Emery blushed as they clinked their glasses together. Their eyes never escaped each other as they took their first sip.

Emery licked her bottom lip before biting it with her teeth. It was clear she was flirting with him. Luca fidgeted in his seat as he thought about how he had almost taken her on her office desk. He sighed, not knowing if he'd be able to make it through lunch without ravaging her.

"So what did Jake say to you to convince you to come all the way to Chicago?"

"Once he told me that there was nothing going on between

you two, it didn't take much convincing. He said you needed help with the pitch."

"He said I needed help?"

"He was worried that the organic idea wasn't going to go over well with Don on its own." Luca tried reading her expression. "But it was obvious you didn't need the help."

"No, I did need the help. He wasn't going for the organic idea. It wasn't until you threatened a big PR scandal that he finally seemed to be listening."

"Yes, but all those facts about consumer statistics and business stuff. You're very good."

"I don't know about that."

"Seriously, Emery. I was amazed."

Emery blushed.

"Anyway, Jake apparently wanted to make things right. Especially since he stole you away from me before giving me a chance to tell my side of the story." He took a long drink of his wine.

"So why did you come to the gala?"

Luca took a breath in. "I came to the gala to talk with Emerson Smith about the negotiations. I thought you were a man."

"What?"

"I didn't know you were you. I assumed … well … anyway, I came to convince you to come to see the plantation for yourself. I thought that maybe if I could get you out of the boardroom, you would be able to see why we wouldn't be able to take another round of price cuts."

Emery tapped her lips with her pointer finger while she took in the information.

"I was not expecting Emerson to be the beautiful conejita

I met on the street during the flower festival. And I was especially not expecting my brother to get in the way and assault you."

"About your brother," Emery paused. "I'm sure it was a very hard decision to turn him in to the police."

"It was." Luca nodded. "But it turned out for the best. Thanks to you for not pressing charges. He was finally able to get the medical help he needed."

"So he's doing better?"

"Yes, but I still haven't completely forgiven him. Especially after what he did to you. Or what he almost …" Luca's words got caught in his throat.

"Everything is okay now." Emery reached her hand across the table, and he took it between his two callused hands and brought it to his lips for a kiss.

They sat together in comforting silence for a while. Emery's fingertips were still cupped in his hand, sending him soothing vibes for his soul. Luca pressed soft kisses on each fingerprint as Emery watched him carefully.

"So what's next for Emerson Smith and the organic coffee business idea?" Luca asked.

"I don't know. If Don is bought in, then he has to convince the board. It's really up to them to decide how to proceed."

"Do you think they'll shut down the CBP division?" Luca asked.

"They may not shut down completely. But hopefully, they'll stop production until they can figure out how to correct their formula."

"I see." Luca frowned.

"And what about you? What's next for Luca Mendoza and the coffee plantation?" Emery asked.

"Well, I'm going to have to hire an office manager. Juan and Mateo are not old enough to pick up the responsibilities, and I need the help." Luca thought about it for a moment, and impulsively spit out his idea. "Why don't you come back with me?" he asked. "You could be the office manager." As soon as Luca said the words, they sounded ridiculous. Emery had the job of her dreams in the city she grew up in. How could he possibly ask her to leave everything behind for him?

Luca looked guiltily at his hands before he looked up to find Emery's eyes shimmering in sadness. He knew the answer before she said it.

"You know I can't just leave here."

Luca held his breath, hoping there was more to her answer, but the silence grew thick and heavy in place of the unsaid things he wished she'd say.

A pizza descended between them and was placed on a pizza stand.

Luca thought he heard the waitress say "Can I get you two anything else?" but he was fixated on Emery's fiery amber eyes. She fidgeted with her napkin nervously before taking her wineglass and tipping the whole thing down her throat.

"Forget I asked."

"Luca. Don't be like that. You saw what I am dealing with here. I have to stay and do everything I can to help the people in Colombia."

"You're right."

Neither of them touched the steaming pizza in front of them.

"Do you want to take this to go?" Emery asked.

Luca nodded.

***

Emery and Luca strolled along the sidewalk of the busy city. The clouds looked heavy in the sky, threatening to dump rain on the peaceful path along the lake.

Emery's heart felt heavy knowing Luca was leaving tomorrow. She snuggled into Luca's arm, hoping that his closeness would comfort her. While they ambled through the park in silence, their hands intertwined. She looked up to find Luca's furrowed brow. His lips pressed together in a straight line. He was disappointed she wouldn't agree to move to Colombia. How could she? She just landed her dream job. Moving to Colombia was out of the question.

"We're here." They arrived at her condo building and approached the elevator in the quiet lobby covered in white marble and black granite tile. Emery pressed the circular button with the number 16 on the elevator keypad when Luca grabbed her hand with a firm grip.

"Looks like we have a long way up," Luca said. His eyes sparkled with mischief.

"We do," Emery said breathlessly.

Luca let the pizza box fall to the ground as he pinned both of Emery's arms over her head, pressing her against the elevator wall. His breath tickled her face as he paused an inch away from her mouth.

Emery's breath grew more rapid, waiting for him to kiss her, but he held her hands securely with one hand and let his other hand trail the length of her body, from her ribs down to the hem of her skirt.

Emery leaned forward to kiss him, but he pulled away, teasing her. The corners of his mouth curled into a wicked, taunting smile before he started unbuttoning her blouse. Emery squirmed, trying to pull her arms down, but his grip held her captive to the sweet torture.

As the last button came undone, Luca brought his finger to Emery's lips, tracing the outline until Emery playfully nipped at him with her teeth. Luca's eyebrow rose tauntingly as he continued to trace his finger down her chin and neck, from her collarbone to the center of her cleavage and down her silky camisole. His fingertip pressed against her skirt until he reached the hem and playfully slid up her leg, finding the lace of her underwear. A few delicate caresses atop the lace fabric had Emery churning with a fiery need for him.

"Please," she heard herself say.

Luca's mouth covered hers, and she gave in to his kiss.

Bing. The elevator doors opened to the sixteenth floor, and Luca released himself from her, leaving her breathless and wanting. Luca picked up the pizza box and took her hand to lead her out of the elevator, giving her a knowing smile before patting her on the butt.

"Lead the way, conejita."

Emery tried composing herself before walking toward her condo. She hated that she loved the control he had on her. She opened her condo door, and Luca stepped in.

"I'll be right back," Emery said with a sinful grin. "Make yourself at home."

***

Luca sat down on the white sofa, sinking into the squeaky leather cushions. Side tables were adorned with crystal vases and potpourri. He picked up one of the little dishes and took a whiff. Vanilla and lavender. A silver picture frame featured an older man with white hair and a full white mustache resting below a kind pair of amber eyes, just like Emery's. He grabbed the frame, shaking the table slightly, and another frame fell forward. He scurried to fix them, before resting his hands in his lap before he broke something.

"Ahem." Emery cleared her throat. Luca looked up to find her in nothing but a creamy silk camisole that fell just below the crease at her hips. Her long legs looked soft and smooth, her hair tousled to one side.

Luca swallowed hard. He was about to get up, but Emery shook her finger at him. She sauntered toward Luca and straddled his hips. She carefully unbuttoned his shirt, tickling his chest with her delicate fingers. Emery unwrapped Luca like a present, exposing his chest and shoulders and placing soft kisses along his collarbone.

"My sweet conejita, you are quite the seductress," Luca said.

Emery gave him a long, sultry kiss, slipping her tongue in his mouth. She pressed into his lap, awakening the deep desire from his loins. Luca wrapped his hands into her hair when she stopped. With a teasing look in her eye, she got up from his lap and walked toward the kitchen. Her little butt cheeks peeked just below her tiny little camisole.

"Can I get you a drink?" she asked, pulling two glasses from the cupboard.

"Sure," Luca laughed, enjoying her little charade as she slinked her way around the kitchen. Her nipples poked through the silky fabric, causing Luca to nearly lose his self-control.

"Scotch?"

He raised his eyebrows. "Yes, gracias."

They clinked their glasses together before taking their first sip. The initial bite of the scotch was soothed by the warm, buttery finish. He watched Emery as she pulled out an ice cube from her glass and walked over to Luca. She pressed the ice cube against Luca's chest, sending a shock of cold through his muscles. Then she followed her tongue behind the icy trail she made along his skin, giving him a fireworks show of sensations.

"Dios mio," Luca panted.

Emery stopped again, plopping the half-melted ice cube back into her glass. Luca watched her, mouth agape, as she backed up against the kitchen counter, lifting herself onto the white-tiled countertop. With a coy smile behind her tumbler glass, she spread her legs for him, beckoning for him to come closer. His heart nearly burst before he could reach her, letting her wrap her long legs around his waist.

Chapter 31

Luca lay awake in bed. He had been watching Emery sleep for hours, but his heart ached. The thought of saying goodbye to her was too much for him to bear. He slipped his arm from under her and sat up in bed. His head rested in his hands as he tried to block out the thoughts of going back to Colombia alone.

He had never dreamed that he could fall in love with anyone, let alone a smart and sophisticated woman like Emery. She came from a completely different world, full of luxurious cotton linens and fancy cocktail parties. He knew it was unfair to ask her to leave the life she has built for herself.

The ache in Luca's heart dripped into his stomach, turning into a tar that burned his insides. He had to get out. Pulling on his pants, he looked over his shoulder at her, angelic in the soft moonglow. As Luca pulled his arms through his shirtsleeve, the ruffling sound stirred Emery awake.

"Are you leaving?" she asked, her voice muffled with sleep.

Luca looked down to find Emery's almond-shaped eyes sparkling with unshed tears.

"I couldn't sleep," Luca said, sitting back down on the edge of the bed. Guilt consumed him, but it was time to leave. Emery reached over and put her hand on his back, but Luca flinched.

"What's wrong?" she asked.

"I can't stay here anymore. It's eating me up inside that I can't have you. Forever."

"Luca, I …"

Luca took her silence as an answer and got up to leave.

"Wait," Emery cried as Luca reached her bedroom door. "I love you."

"Then come back with me to Colombia."

"You know I can't." Emery said, tears streaming down her face.

"I understand," Luca said. He turned to leave.

"Can't we talk about this?" Emery's words tugged on his already broken heart.

"Goodbye, conejita."

"Luca," Emery whimpered.

It took everything in Luca's willpower to not turn and comfort her. He could hear her gentle sobs from the bedroom as he stopped in the kitchen. He reached in his pocket to pull out the wooden figurine, placing it on the counter before he left.

Chapter 32

Emery sat down at her desk. She sipped her coffee, reading over quality reports from the last quarter. She looked up to see Jake walk into his office. The light flicked on, and his briefcase clicked open.

It had been three weeks since their pitch to Don, without a word. Emery had agonized over every detail of their presentation, not knowing if she had convinced Don to stop the negotiations and the CBP pesticide production or not.

Jake had become distant, giving Emery her space after she had reprimanded him for pulling a stunt like flying Luca to Chicago without her consent. To come to her rescue, of all things! It was downright insulting. Even though she knew his intention was good, she made it clear to him that he had overstepped his boundaries. Jake had stopped swinging by her office ever since. Part of her missed their camaraderie, but the other part knew the distance between them was for the best.

Jeanine appeared from behind the door. "Excuse me, but Don needs to see you right away."

"Is it about the pitch?" Emery stood abruptly. Her heart raced.

"Not sure." Jeanine shrugged and sat back down at her desk.

"Did he need Jake too?" Emery called out through the

window.

"Not this time," Jeanine said as she continued to type on her computer.

It was finally Judgment Day. Emery wasn't sure if she was approaching a firing squad or not, yet she walked briskly to Don's office, the anxiety building with every step forward.

She approached his door and walked in. Don ushered her to sit down.

"How did it go with the board?"

Don looked up over his spectacles. "Emerson, despite the stunt you pulled in Colombia and the fact that you threatened this company with a huge PR scandal …" Don stood. The heavy crease in his forehead deepened with his frown. "The board found your presentation material to be very convincing. They want to get started on the organic thing right away."

"What? Really?" Emery's eyes grew wide. Did she really just hear what she thought she heard?

"So here's the deal. We'll need a staff in the Medellín office to ensure the farmers are establishing organic practices. The board approved one president-level head located here in Chicago to start the new division. Do you know anyone who might be interested in the position?"

Emery stared at him in disbelief.

"I was thinking since this was your brainchild that maybe you would be interested in the role."

"Wow. I don't know what to say. Can I think about it?"

"Of course. And oh, by the way, marketing asked if we could get a Colombian male model for our new organic branding. I was thinking we could ask that handsome gentleman that was here. What was his name?"

Emery froze in her chair. "Luca Mendoza?"

"Yes, that's him. Call him up and have him submit a few headshots. He's perfect. Rugged. Handsome. And an actual freakin' coffee farmer."

"Um. I'm not sure he would be—"

"Of course he would be interested. You can tell him I'm willing to offer him a $200,000 contract for the first year as the face of our new organic coffee brand."

"You want him to be the *face* of our new organic coffee?"

"And I want you to run the whole thing. You've got the brains and the know-how."

Emery stood in shock. Did he just say he wanted her to run the whole thing? Her heart pounded in her ears at the prospect of talking to Luca on the phone. There had been countless times she had picked up the phone to talk to him, but she knew it would have ended in heartbreak. But now, with this offer, he could potentially live here in Chicago, and they would have a chance to be together. And she would be *president* of their organic division? The flutter in her stomach made her giggle. She could not believe it. It was almost too good to be true.

"Sir, may I ask what the board decided to do about the CBP division?"

"What about it?" Don cleared his throat. "I just offered you and Mendoza very lucrative positions at this company and you're going to pester me about CBP?"

Emery clenched her teeth. Her balloon of hope burst as Don waved her off. He wasn't offering her a president position because she deserved it; he was offering her a bribe.

"Don, with all due respect, the CBP division just needs to pause production until—"

"Let me handle the CBP division. All right? I don't want to hear another word about it. I suggest you think very hard about this once-in-a-lifetime opportunity. You hear me? Now bring that handsome coffee farmer back to me, and give me an answer on your job offer by the end of week."

Emery gave a weak nod and slipped out of the office.

Chapter 33

It had been a month since Luca left Chicago, but his heart was still heavy with sadness as he got out of bed that morning. A pulsating headache emerged as he stood up, and he looked at the half-empty bottle of rum on his nightstand as if it were personally responsible for his morning ache.

Luca walked over to the mirror. The ashy hue to his skin and the dark circles under his eyes gave away a late night of drinking alone, wallowing in self-pity. He would need a couple of hours before he could check in on Juan and Mateo. They didn't need to see him like this.

Luca slipped a white T-shirt over his head and pulled his jeans on. He stepped into his boots and walked out his front door to get some fresh air.

The sun was hidden behind a heavy layer of fog that covered the mountain and pooled in the valley of coffee trees. The sound of rain in the distance drew nearer. Birds flew out from the trees in the valley to escape the downpour.

The first raindrops tickled his nose and collected above his thick eyelashes. A moment later, the rain clouded his vision. Luca stood still, engulfed in Mother Earth's tears. He found comfort under the pressure of the rain on his chest and shoulders; it was like nature's way of giving him a hug.

I am sorry for your broken heart, said the rain.

He walked through the trees, sinking into the mud, stepping on the saturated ground. He inspected the cherries, a perfect shade of red, ready to be picked. Raphael would normally schedule the pickers, but he was still at the institute. Luca would have to organize the next harvest himself. He cursed himself for not thinking to do it sooner and stomped his way up to the office.

As he trudged up the hill in the pouring rain, he saw someone standing in front of his office door—a woman wearing a white dress, soaked from the unrelenting rain. She was peeking into the office window and then turned to leave.

Emery?

She spotted him, and their eyes locked through the downpour.

Luca quickened his pace as Emery stepped off the porch. She ran to Luca.

"Luca!" she said before he took her in his arms.

"What are you doing here?" Luca asked, cupping her face. Her cheeks and nose were rosy from the cool air.

"I was offered a new position at Coffee Benz," Emery said. "But before I made the decision, I wanted to see if your offer to be your office manager was still on the table."

Luca smiled. Unshed tears welled in the corners of his eyes. She looked up at him with so much hope, his heart nearly burst with joy.

"Of course it is," he said. "But I can tell you right now it wouldn't pay a fraction of your other offer."

"Yes, but your offer has better benefits." She smiled.

"Benefits?"

"Assuming you are a part of the package."

"Me?" Luca asked, pretending like he didn't know what she was talking about.

"Of course you. That is, if you'll have me."

He stared into the depths of her eyes for a long time before he could get the strength to let his tears go with the rain. She pulled his face to him and kissed him softly.

"Are you really here? Or am I dreaming?"

"Yes, I'm here. And I'm yours." She pressed light kisses on his mouth, kissing his lips, his nose, his chin. Her lips were slick and shivering in the rain. Luca picked her up and tossed her over his shoulder.

Emery squealed. "Luca! Where are you taking me?"

"I'm getting you out of this rain. Plus, your nipples are showing again." Luca laughed.

"You brute!" Emery swatted his backside as he ran across the field with her rump in the air. Luca opened the door to his living room and set her down. The sound of the rain reverberated against Luca's windows. Emery's breath picked up as Luca slipped her dress off her shoulders, letting it clump to the floor.

Emery started to unbutton his shirt and stopped halfway through.

"Wait," she said. "I can't accept your offer."

Luca froze. "Qué?"

"I'm sorry, I can't be your office manager. I have big dreams. I have plans for myself, and for the future," Emery said as she walked across the room. She picked up his phone, dialed a number and waited for a moment.

What is happening? Luca was dumbstruck as Emery twirled the phone cord around her finger as she waited for someone to pick up the other line. Her cotton lingerie had become translucent, wreaking havoc on Luca's nerves.

"Hi, yes, is Don there?" she said, looking away from Luca as she sat down in his reclining chair and crossed her long legs.

"Hi, Don? It's Emery. I have considered your job offer, and I have to respectfully decline the position. I've decided to start my own organic coffee business instead. And given that I'm officially a competitor, I understand that my employment with Coffee Benz ends now."

She paused to look over at Luca, who stood in awe.

"Oh now, don't get your panties in a bunch. A woman-owned coffee company is the least of your worries. The press is what you should really be worried about, especially when they find out you tried to bribe us into keeping quiet about CBP. See you in the news, Don."

Emery hung up and spun the reclining chair, revealing the most mischievous, adorable grin.

"I'm sorry, Luca. As I mentioned earlier, I can't accept your office manager role after all. However, I would like to make an offer to you. Will you be the first coffee plantation to be a part of my new organic coffee company?" She playfully caught her fingernail with her teeth and smiled brightly.

"You continue to amaze me." Luca smiled. He walked over to the beautiful woman sitting in his chair and picked her up. Her arms wrapped around his neck as he carried her off to his bedroom.

"And what are you going to name your new coffee company?" Luca asked, resting her on his mattress.

"Hmm. I was thinking something along the lines of Conejita Coffee Company," Emery said proudly, pulling his face toward her.

"It has a nice ring to it." Luca smiled. "But what was this

bribe that you turned down on my behalf?"

"For you, it was a $200,000 contract as the face of their new organic coffee division, that I was going to lead."

"Whoa there, wait a minute. $200,000? I didn't agree to turn down that much money."

"You can't be serious." Emery shot up, her eyes wild.

Luca gave her a sly grin, wrapping his arms tightly around her, basking in Emery's gullibility.

Emery playfully slapped the dimples off of Luca's face. "You are so naughty!"

"And you are so sweet. My sweet conejita," Luca said as he planted a kiss on Emery's lips.

Acknowledgments

This book would not be possible without my sister. Kweek, thank you for helping me get this book off the ground. Your ideas and contributions gave this story so much more color and life. Words cannot express how much I appreciate your part in the process.

I'd like to thank my copy editor, Alexandra Ott, and proofreader, Beth Attwood, for whipping my debut novel into shape. To my amazing cover photographer and designer, Erik Ebeling, you nailed it! Thank you for the gorgeous work, and your meticulous attention to detail. I can only hope my book is living up to the cover.

Special thanks to my beta reader, Maria Lanning, for reading this book before it was ready, and for supporting me along the way!

Last but not least, thank you to my loving and supporting husband, children, parents, in-laws, family and friends for all your encouragement. Without you, I wouldn't have stuck with it, and for that, I'm eternally grateful.

About the Author

Alicia Crofton is a romance novelist and a sucker for a good love story. She lives with her husband and two children, nestled in Portland, Oregon's jungle of roses.

Join her mailing list for updates on upcoming books.

You can connect with me on:
- http://www.aliciacrofton.com
- http://www.facebook.com/aliciacroftonauthor
- https://www.instagram.com/aliciacroftonauthor

Subscribe to my newsletter:
- https://mailchi.mp/31aee60d4ff1/aliciacroftonsignup

Also by Alicia Crofton

To My Muse, With Love
Nora Miller, an aspiring writer, struggles to come up with a book idea. Inspiration strikes when she meets Kellen Atwood, the mysterious coffee shop guy who saves her from disaster one minute and vanishes the next.

Years later, Nora's published book, *Coffee, My Love*, is adapted for the big screen. She meets the charming producer, Jack Crawford, who sweeps her off her feet. Her dreams were coming true, until she runs into the dark stranger from her past. The muse who inspired her story. The one who left her in the dust.

Nora's determined to not let Hot Coffee Shop Guy get under her skin again, but her heart has other plans.